Flight Risk

Rayanne Sinclair

Hopetoun Publishing
Edmonds, Washington

Rayanne Sinclair

FLIGHT RISK
Rayanne Sinclair

HOPETOUN PUBLISHING
Edmonds, Washington

For more information about this and other books by Rayanne Sinclair, visit www.rayannesinclair.com

Print ISBN 978-0-9897502-6-4
Electronic ISBN 978-09897502-7-1

This is dedicated to the ones who know me

Acknowledgements

Thanks again to Nancy Wick (developmental editor), Beth Jusino (publications consultant), Jenn Reese (cover artist), Laura Vowles (primary beta reader), Stephanie Cooper (proofreader), and Kathy Burge (copyeditor) for contributing their talents to this novella. These wonderful women have been involved in some or all of my previous works. I do hope that it won't be the last time I get to work with these gifted helpers.

Lastly, I want to thank my husband, Dave, who has stood by me during all of my publications. I'm certain I could never have a more loyal and supportive person in my life.

Chapter 1

"Stieglitz is dead," declared flight nurse Prudhoe Bonner as her eye caught the small photo taped to the cockpit panel of what she figured was the dead pilot's wife.

"What the hell do we do now?" copilot Joe Metz shouted while trying to stabilize the airplane.

"First priority—you'd better prepare for the potential of having to fly this plane alone. Meanwhile, I'll do my best to find someone in back who can pull the pilot out of his seat and help you land in Anchorage," said Prudhoe, struggling to remain calm.

Young and still somewhat inexperienced, Metz had never encountered such a serious problem, and Prudhoe could see he wasn't holding up well under the pressure. There were only seven passengers on this flight, but she knew there were plenty of bush pilots in Alaska. She hoped she'd get lucky.

"Anyone here have a pilot's license?" Prudhoe shouted loud enough to be heard above the engine noise in the small cabin.

The largest individual on the flight, who looked to be about six feet two inches tall and two hundred pounds, unbuckled his seat belt to make his way toward the front. He never answered Prudhoe's question, bulling past her in the aisle. Once in the cockpit, he found the pilot's slumped body. With Metz pushing himself up against the far side of the cockpit, the stranger reached inside the small space and proceeded to release the seat slide and seat belt to pull the pilot's limp body into the narrow aisleway. Panic-stricken passengers gasped and stared wide-eyed.

Over the audible sobbing of one female passenger, Prudhoe yelled back to the stranger, "You know what you're doing with this machine?"

"Yes, ma'am, I'll take it from here. You take care of that sick kid in the rear."

Prudhoe wanted to do nothing more than return to the low-hanging bed cage behind the thin white curtain separating her twelve-year-old patient from the single-side passenger seats up front. Pale as death, Christian Snyder was being transported from Juneau to Anchorage with life-threatening injuries from a hunting accident. By the time Prudhoe returned to her heavily medicated patient, she found the boy's mother in tears.

"Any changes in my absence?" she asked the distraught mother.

"No, but what's going on up there? I'm scared to death about losing my son, and now I'm scared to death that this plane will go down. Flying isn't something I do every day."

"Mrs. Snyder, calm down—for your sake and for the sake of your son, who can probably hear what's being said. We're all gonna be fine, and I'm determined to get Christian safely into the hands of the professionals in Anchorage. Got it?"

Prudhoe wasn't about to admit that she didn't know if any of them were going to make it, given the weather report she'd heard on the radio while she was checking on the dead pilot. She wondered if that big fellow in the dead pilot's seat knew what he had signed up for.

With the plane once again running level and rising closer to its service ceiling for this portion of the flight, the passengers appeared to be a bit more at ease. But there was still no word from the cockpit as to current status, and Prudhoe figured the ease might last only another minute if someone didn't get on the horn to tell everyone what was going on.

No sooner did that thought cross her mind than she heard the crackling of the cabin's public address system—and then the voice of Joe Metz, sounding a bit calmer now.

"Ladies and gentlemen, this is your copilot. We've experienced a serious event in the cockpit. Yes, what you see in the aisleway is the pilot, who suddenly passed away at the helm. However, a fellow passenger has stepped forward to help—a licensed pilot with flight experience. Please remain calm and stay fastened into your seats as we complete our flight into Anchorage International Airport. We're just about an hour out. Thank you for your attention."

Prudhoe looked over at Mrs. Snyder to see if she registered a calmer demeanor after the announcement, but no go. The mother's hands were shaking on her lap as she studied her son's still body. Meanwhile, all Prudhoe could think about was what Metz hadn't mentioned in his announcement.

CHAPTER 2

Despite the turbulence and a hard but successful landing in Anchorage the day before, Prudhoe was back into her early morning routine. Carrying her strong black coffee to the dinette in her small apartment, her eyes glanced at the front page of the *Anchorage Daily Times* she'd pulled off the porch. There it was—the May 10, 1959, front-page article about the hero who landed a small plane that was transferring a young patient to the hospital in town. She recognized the tall and handsome fellow in the picture as the man who took the pilot seat yesterday. The photo of him standing alone in his parka and ear-flapped corduroy hat was in the center of the article, and it looked like it may have been taken inside the terminal hangar.

Mentally resisting her flashback of fear from the flight, Prudhoe scanned the story content and found a quote from the copilot.

"The Model 10 Electra really needs a second crew member, and we found it in this passenger who came forward at just the right time. Pacific Alaska Airways is grateful to Braedon Clarkson for saving the remaining lives on board. Our condolences go out to Mrs. Stieglitz for the tragic loss of her husband, a skilled pilot who had been with the company for nearly ten years."

According to the article, the thirty-two-year-old Braedon Clarkson was a skilled hunter, dog musher, wilderness guide, and bush pilot. It was also reported that he'd recently obtained his associate's degree from the University of Alaska and was employed by the General Land Office in Anchorage.

A shiver went up her spine as she recalled the plunging plane that was righted but then faced rough weather after that.

"Damn," she whispered, as she took another sip of coffee. Sitting in her oversized men's flannel bathrobe, she glanced out the small window, staring at the typical gray skies. For a fleeting moment, she let herself consider the potential of having never seen this new day. At age twenty-nine, she couldn't remember a time when she'd come this close to death, outside of the earthquake and tsunami the previous year. The whole thing made her anxious, wondering if the gods of nature were angry...maybe even with her.

Pushing away from the table, Prudhoe made her way back to the kitchen to toss her remaining coffee in the sink and place the mug on the counter with her growing pile of dirty dishes. As she looked at the clock on the wall, she calculated it was too late to wash dishes now.

"Gotta get dressed and get to work," she muttered to herself.

Day shift was new to Prudhoe this year, having spent several years on nights. As she stepped into the shower and let the water warm her cold but flawless light brown skin, she thought about how much better she liked working day shift. It left evenings for fun on the town. However, feeling beat from hard days at work Sundays through Thursdays meant her time to enjoy life was left to Friday and Saturday nights. Trying not to get her hair wet, she was already looking forward to Friday night tavern time with friends.

Drying off, she rolled her long, straight raven-black hair into a bun. Then she gathered up a few more bobby pins to secure her white nursing cap before leaving the apartment. White hose, her plain front-button shirt dress, and sensible gum sole white shoes were awaiting her in the small closet. By six thirty, she had donned her coat and begun the half-mile walk to the hospital on this crisp forty degree May morning.

Chapter 3

No sooner had Prudhoe checked in at the intensive care nurses station than she heard the bell from room four. She set her lunch bag down under the desk and waved to the charge nurse on duty, who was just coming out of room six further down the hallway. Well, at least her boss knew she had made it to work a few minutes before shift change, even if she hadn't seen the nurse she was to relieve yet.

"How's my boy this morning?" Prudhoe inquired of her supervisor.

"Christian? Still pretty groggy since coming back here from recovery about ten hours ago," said the charge nurse as she sat down at the station. "Doc's still worried about infection and nerve damage, but the wound looks good this morning—just redressed about an hour ago."

Entering room four, Prudhoe was startled to see the patient sitting up. It wasn't often that the patients on this wing could even use the call button because of the severity of their conditions. However, Mrs. Carter was due to be transferred to the regular medical floor today anyway. Seemed she was a bit anxious and simply wanted to know what the plan was for her on this day.

"Mrs. C., you should be lying down. I know you're eager to get outta here, but you're still all hooked up, and we've got some work to do to untether you. Besides, Dr. Hazlet has to sign off on your chart and provide instructions to the medical floor nurses you'll be delivered to later. You're up early—can I get you some breakfast?"

Mrs. Carter sighed heavily, which was actually something Prudhoe was happy to hear. After all, this patient had been on a respirator up until just a week ago.

"Nurse Bonner, I'm altogether too familiar with the hospital's cuisine, and I'm not sure I can deal with it anymore. Is it any better on the floor you're sending me to?" she inquired with a weak smile.

"I'm afraid not, Mrs. C. Same chef, same dietitians, same food. However, you'll probably get a wider variety than you've seen here as of late. Let me see what I can hunt down for you this morning... and I already know about your tea preference."

Lying back down, Mrs. Carter pulled the white sheet and covers to her shoulders as she tucked herself in. Prudhoe returned to the nurse's station to call the kitchen in hopes of catching them before trays were sent up this morning.

After making her morning rounds, Prudhoe stood in the hallway to complete some notes before placing the chart back in room one and heading to see Christian Snyder. But on her way, she noticed a familiar figure walking toward her, wearing a black pea coat over dark trousers and a white button-down shirt and tie. Wait just a minute—that was the guy from the airlift flight yesterday, she realized.

"Good morning, Nurse Bonner," came the greeting from none other than the big hero, Braedon Clarkson.

"Good morning, ace. What brings you back into my world... or was yesterday not eventful enough for you?" asked Prudhoe.

"Well, I was heading to work this morning and thought I'd stop by to see how the patient is doing. Am I allowed to do that?"

"Usually just immediate family, but follow me. I haven't seen him yet this morning, but I suspect you're not going to get too much reaction given all the meds in him right now. It's nice of you to take the time to visit, but you'd be better off returning in a few days."

"I just might have to do that," Braedon said in a lower tone as they entered Christian's room together.

As Prudhoe reached the bedside and began her routine of checking the drip lines and monitors, Braedon just stared at the young boy, who didn't even open his eyes. Neither did Mrs. Snyder, as she lay slumped in the chair next to Christian this morning. Not wanting to disturb either one, the two slipped out quietly after Prudhoe made some notes on the chart at the end of the bed.

Prudhoe was the first to break the silence with, "I saw the article in the paper this morning. Looks like you're the man of the hour. I was so focused on getting Christian and his mom to the transporter that I didn't have a chance to thank you for saving all our lives yesterday."

"Wasn't aiming to be a hero, Nurse. Just trying to get us all home in one piece."

"Well, you did just that. Thank you!"

"Listen, I think I will take you up on a return visit in a few days when the little guy is more alert. Will you be around?" asked Braedon.

"Well, even though it feels like I live here, I'm not here all the time. So if you want to make the visit in the morning, I'm here Sundays through Thursdays. You might want to shoot for Thursday morning. Kids bounce back pretty quick, and I expect he'll be wide awake, staring at the morning cartoons on the television."

"Great. I'll make my way back to your world on Thursday then. And by the way, it's you folks here who are in the life-saving business. Thanks for what you do, Nurse Bonner. Oh, I never caught your first name."

"Prudhoe... Prudhoe Bonner," she replied, while still reeling from his statement. In fact, Prudhoe couldn't remember a time someone other than a patient or family member had thanked her for doing her job. She loved nursing and was good at it. Good enough to be chosen for specialized training in airlift situations last year. Yesterday's flight was only her fifth, but not one she figured she'd ever forget.

"See you in a few days, Prudhoe."

Chapter 4

Busy when at work and tired at night, Prudhoe had forgotten all about the hospital visitor from earlier in the week. That is, until she saw Braedon Clarkson walking down the hall again toward her on Thursday morning around eight o'clock. This time she had her hands full with a patient they were about to receive from the emergency ward downstairs.

Braedon was all smiles until he heard the clacking gurney coming around the corner and the orderlies speaking loudly to each other over the din. He stood out of the way and up against the wall as he watched Prudhoe and another nurse direct the activity into one of the rooms that swallowed all of them when she closed the door behind her.

Braedon wasn't sure if he should proceed alone to room six to see Christian or sit in the small visitor waiting room down the hall until Prudhoe reappeared. Not in a hurry to get to the office, he made the decision to wait for a bit to see what happened. After all, it was just him and Jim Wright that made up the new outpost office for land management. Jim would be at the office by now, but Braedon had indicated he'd be in a bit later today because of this hospital visit.

Everything about Alaskan land management, mineral rights, and homesteading was in flux in the face of statehood and the feds down in Washington, D.C. But Braedon wasn't too concerned, given that he'd already put in forty-five hours of work this week, and it was only Thursday.

Sitting in the glassed-in waiting room and twirling his hat on his index finger, Braedon was deep in thought about the workday ahead when he saw Prudhoe exit the patient room. She made a beeline to the nurses station to place a call and then headed back into the room as fast as her white-soled shoes would carry her. He sat back in the stiff chair and let his mind wander to Prudy's beautiful hair with the little nursing cap on the top. For just a second, he caught himself thinking about her tiny waistline cinched up in her crisp white shirtdress. Before long, he began to question his motives in coming to see the young boy. After all, he had been rather taken with this petite, dark beauty the moment he brushed by her on the plane last weekend.

Shaking off the thoughts in his head, he stood up and began heading to room six to see Christian. Just then the door to the seriously ill patient opened, and the hospital staff poured out of the room. The last one out was Nurse Bonner, who closed the door behind her and made eye contact with Braedon.

"Hey, handsome, back to see Christian? I gotta say I wasn't sure you'd actually return, but he's doing lots better this morning. Stick your head in and meet his mother. She'll want to thank you, I'm sure."

Braedon was taken aback by her casual banter, particularly in light of the emergency she had just been involved in.

"How do you stay so cool in this kind of work environment? You're amazing," said Braedon.

"Look who's talking, Mr. Cool, who takes over for the pilot in midair and lands safely as though it was an everyday thing."

"Well, it's not an everyday thing for me, but you have to face life and death each day...probably each hour."

"Yeah, we assess and react quickly—but it's our training. The hard part is when we lose people. It beats the stuffing out of us. Still, it comes with the territory. Speaking of territory—how's the land management business these days?"

"Evolving, but things are going well. Hey, do you have time to introduce me to Mrs. Snyder? I feel kind of odd just walking into the room unannounced."

"Sure," responded Prudhoe as she escorted Braedon to the boy's room.

After introductions, during which Mrs. Snyder broke down in tears while thanking both the nurse and Clarkson, Christian piped up, begging to hear all about what happened when he was unaware of what was going on. As Braedon retold the story of events on board the plane that day, Prudhoe's thoughts momentarily wandered again to the prospect of death—something she greatly feared, despite her external calm in the face of it.

As the two departed the room, Braedon touched Prudhoe on the arm to get her attention. Looking directly into his dark brown eyes, which matched his slicked-back thick brown hair, it was as though she really saw him for the first time.

"Thanks for accompanying me in there. May I call you sometime, Prudhoe?"

Focused on his eyes, she replied, "Ah, sure...I mean, yes. Let me write down my phone number."

Heading to the nurses station, she tore a piece of paper from a chart notepad and wrote down her number on the blank backside.

Taking the paper, he smiled and noted her small handwriting taking up just a corner of the page. Folding it several times, he tucked it away in his jacket and began making his way back down the hall, past the visitor waiting room.

Prudhoe was left staring at the back of him as he departed. On his way to the elevator, he heard the call bell going off again.

Chapter 5

That same Thursday night found Prudhoe downtown at her favorite tavern. It was beer-musty, dark, and the men outnumbered the women five to one. This was her hunting ground when it came to meeting men, even though she already knew many of them. She never thought of herself as being their prey because she was the one who had control over them. Given that she was a British Columbia Nuxalk Nation beauty weighing in at 120 pounds on her five-foot-five frame, she was right about that.

Flirting with a newcomer that she'd not seen in the bar before, she had him eating out of her hand... quite literally, as she shelled peanuts and popped them in his mouth. He'd already had too much to drink and had his arm around her as they sat in the booth.

"Did you say you're a nurse?" he slurred.

"Yep, down the road at the local hospital."

"Hey, I'd be willing to get myself sick or hurt just to see you in action. I'll bet you look pretty in your white uniform. How 'bout you take me to your place and show me what you look like in that."

"Keep eating; you need to get food in your stomach to slow the effects of the alcohol. And I have a policy of only bringing sober guys home with me. After all, I can't be sure the drunken ones can perform."

"Aw, you should give me a try, Nurse. I'm not as drunk as you think."

Prudhoe moved his arm off her shoulder and excused herself from the table, saying she had to use the restroom. Her real plan was to ditch the guy and head home since it was already midnight.

She flipped some change onto the bar and winked at the owner on her way out the back door. Billy had witnessed Prudhoe's catch-and-release routine before. Apparently, she'd chosen to throw this one back.

Arriving back at her apartment, she decided to take a long, hot shower to wash off the tavern as well as to warm up. Twilight had passed about thirty minutes ago, and though it would be light again in just a few hours, her body knew it needed sleep. As she slipped into bed that night, she felt a bit sorry for the guy she left at the table, but not too much. Acknowledging that it was pleasant to have a warm man next to her, she felt a bit smug about what she considered to be her selectiveness when it came to men. However, as she drifted off to sleep, she also had to acknowledge that she'd never selected one that had turned out to be a decent prospect.

Prudhoe usually slept in until around noon on Saturdays, but the phone rang at eight o'clock. Groaning, she dragged herself out of bed to the small kitchen. Picking up the heavy black phone receiver, she heard the voice of the charge nurse on the other end.

"Prudhoe, Nolee is out sick, and we're short-staffed. Can you get into work this morning?"

"Why me? Isn't Rita around?"

"Nope, she's gone to visit a family member at her village this weekend. You gotta help us out, Prudhoe. Besides, it's extra pay for the week."

"Okay, okay, give me thirty minutes, and I'll be there."

Actually arriving at the hospital a bit closer to nine o'clock, Prudhoe was feeling rather put-upon. After all, this was the sixth time this year she'd been called to work outside her regular shift. She didn't mind the additional income, but it definitely put a crimp in her style because she knew she'd not be on the town later tonight.

As she reached the nurses station, the charge nurse was already giving her orders. Apparently, things were pretty hectic on the floor today. Prudhoe immediately slipped into her work mode, spending several hours on her feet before getting a break for lunch. Her thirty-minute meal period didn't give her an opportunity to go home for lunch, so she headed to the cafeteria downstairs. Over the noisy chatter and the clanging metal trays in the small cafeteria, Prudhoe broke bread with friends from the X-ray and lab units before heading back to her floor.

They'd lost a patient in the morning, so folks were pretty quiet on the floor. So much so that the second shift charge nurse said that she could leave at four o'clock that afternoon and still get paid for a full shift. Prudhoe grabbed her coat from the station and made a dash for home, where she could hear the phone ringing just as she was getting her keys out to open the front door. She dropped everything to catch the phone in the middle of the sixth ring.

"Hello."

"Whoa, I was just about to hang up! Prudhoe, this is Braedon Clarkson. Have I caught you at a bad time?"

"Hello, Braedon. Yes... Uh, I mean no... It's a fine time. I almost didn't make it to the phone because I am just getting home from work."

"I thought this was your day off?"

"Yes, they had me working fill-in today because of high census and someone out ill."

"Oh, I see. Well, I'm guessing you're too tired to make dinner for yourself, so perhaps you'll let me take you out to eat tonight? Maybe some fried chicken at the Bone?"

"I'd love to. That sounds so good, and I am so tired after six days of work."

"Great, I'd be glad to pick you up unless you would prefer to meet there."

"Let me change out of this uniform, grab my truck, and meet you there in twenty minutes. How's that?"

"Sounds good. See you there."

Chapter 6

The truck wasn't cooperating this evening. As Prudhoe put her feet on the gas and clutch one more time, it lurched and then died. Letting out a deep breath of exasperation, she grabbed her handbag and went back into her apartment to call the Lucky Wishbone restaurant.

"Hello, I'm calling to ask you guys for a favor. My name is Prudhoe Bonner, and I was supposed to be meeting a man who is on his way to dinner there. He is a big guy with brown hair—last name is Clarkson. When you see him, can you tell him my truck broke down, and I can't make it?"

The tentative female voice on the other end of the phone offered a weak "Yeah, sure thing. What was your last name again?"

After hanging up the phone, Prudhoe walked over to the television to turn it on and then sunk down into the broken-down pads of her old couch. Being pretty sure that she'd ruined her chances of ever getting to know Braedon, she reclined and soon found herself dozing off.

Within ten minutes of sleep, the phone rang again. Braedon was calling from the restaurant, asking Prudhoe where he could pick her up. It was a quick conversation, and after she hung up, she had to concede that the man was persistent.

Running a brush through her hair and dabbing her lips with a greasy balm, Prudhoe was at curbside the moment Braedon's truck appeared to rescue the date. As he idled the vehicle, she didn't hesitate a moment to let herself in on the passenger side. While Prudhoe slid into the old truck, Braedon began making apologies for not having thought through the sharing of phone numbers in the event that an emergency like this occurred.

"Don't worry about it. I appreciate your willingness to come and get me. I don't know about you, but I'm thoroughly hungry. Let's eat!" proclaimed Prudhoe with her usual assertiveness. It was one of the things that Braedon found simultaneously curious and endearing about the lovely nurse.

"With the scent of fried chicken still on me from walking into that place, I think we're both ready to eat," he responded cheerfully.

As he turned the truck around in the center of the road and headed back into town, Prudhoe had a moment to study the man. She tried not to be too obvious about her staring, but it was as though she was finally getting a good long look at him. Their previous meetings had been brief and involved so many distractions. She couldn't help but notice his handsome face, which seemed to feature those deep brown eyes. His thick brown hair was combed back to one side with the part on the right. As her eyes traveled to his arms and down to his hands, she noted their strength as he gripped the steering wheel.

"So you are left with only tomorrow as your day off this time around?" inquired Braedon in an apparent attempt to jump-start the conversation.

"Yeah, I'm gonna sleep in 'til I can't sleep anymore. How 'bout you? Do you sometimes work on the weekends?"

"I have gone into the office on Saturdays, but it's rare. If I have to do that, it's usually to drive out to do a visual on a land use issue. And I don't typically do that outside of this season due to the weather-related road hazards. But I don't ever work on Sundays. It's definitely my day for church and rest. A body needs that."

"I know my body needs rest, but I'll pass on the church attendance. Heck, I think that would probably just put me to sleep anyway," Prudhoe chimed in.

As she finished her sentence, Braedon was pulling into the parking lot and had located a space. Turning the truck around to back into the space, he was looking out the back window and through the gun rack.

"Not interested in the things of God then?"

"Well, I wouldn't put it that way—that sounds kinda harsh. It's just that I'm more than capable of seeing the hand of God when I'm outdoors. I see him in nature."

Braedon didn't respond but jumped out of the truck to come around to get the door for Prudhoe. She wasn't used to this kind of "lady treatment," and it made her a bit uncomfortable. But nothing compared to where their conversation seemed to be going this evening.

As the couple walked into the restaurant, the hostess seemed to light up with the realization that the nice gentleman who had used her phone earlier had actually returned.

"Glad you came back and that you connected with your missing party. Follow me," the young lady said, as she grabbed two menus and led them to a booth near the rear of the restaurant.

As they settled into their booth and reviewed the menu, the familiar sounds of clanging dishes and smells of home cooking made for a relaxing setting. In fact, Prudhoe was feeling so comfortable that the minute the waitress took their order and departed, she jumped back into the former conversation.

"A church man, eh? Where do you go for church around here?"

"The old wooden Methodist church in town. Lots of good folks there. I think you should join me sometime!"

"I think we might want to avoid this subject altogether... if we're going to get along, that is."

Braedon lowered his head a bit and stared at her for a moment before asking, "So just how do we get to know each other better when I'm not allowed to discuss a central theme in my life?"

Prudhoe was impressed. After all, he had a point, and he'd made it gently. His direct yet kind ways made her wonder if this guy was different from the rest. After all, she was good at putting all men into the same basket, though she secretly hoped that there might be at least one who was different. That is, a man who wasn't simply after one thing.

"I hear you. You talk about whatever you want. Just don't be surprised if I'm not interested."

"What are you interested in, Prudhoe?" Braedon inquired.

"My work, my hobby, my fun."

"Tell me more about all of those," he prompted.

"Okay, let's talk about my work. It's not always fun, but I think I'm pretty good at it. I am so glad I had the opportunity to get more nursing education and training through the Indian Health Service. I hope I never stop learning. And my hobby is beading. I especially like to make jewelry using beads and such."

"Ah, did you make that lovely number you're wearing?" Braedon asked as he looked more closely at the beautiful metal medallion hanging from a beaded chain of black, white, red, and silver pieces.

"Well, the metal piece was given to me by a friend, so I made it into this necklace. You like it?"

"Yes, very much. You obviously have a real talent there—an artistic eye. Something I have no skill with. In fact, I can't even draw a stick figure to look like a stick figure!"

"Oh, come now, you're probably too hard on yourself. I think everyone has an artistic spirit within. You just need to find yours."

"Okay, now tell me about what you do for fun?"

"That's kind of personal, don't you think?" Prudhoe asked with a wink.

"I don't know. Is it?" he asked.

"Well, let's just say I like my friends and enjoy meeting them in our favorite watering hole on the weekends."

Interrupted by the waitress who came to take their order, Braedon requested two chicken dinners and then picked up the conversation where Prudhoe had left off.

"So you meet your friends for drinks on the weekends. Did I get that?"

"Yep. But don't get me wrong; I don't get drunk. Saw enough of that growing up. My so-called father was an alky—took off when I was just eight years old. That sent my mother to the bottle, so I had to grow up fast and pretty much on my own."

"I'm sorry to hear that, Prudhoe. It's a serious problem for the native people. Tell me more about yourself."

"Well, I'm not from one of the local clans. They welcome me in and often don't even care that I'm not from Alaska. But I am actually mixed race—Nuxalk and white. My people are from the Bella Coola Valley in British Columbia. And my dad was white, not native. So excessive drinking is a serious problem for lots of people. I know; I see it in the hospital."

"True, and I'm sorry to have implied otherwise. I don't come from a family of drinkers. I can only image how difficult that must have been for you."

"I survived. I was a tough kid. Still am."

Before long, the waitress brought their meals, and they were ready to dive in. However, Prudhoe wasn't altogether sure what to do when Braedon bowed his head over the meal in silent prayer. She felt uncomfortable but decided to wait to eat out of respect.

CHAPTER 7

As he sat in the pew of the dilapidated church on Sunday, Braedon contemplated the dinner date from the night before. Prudhoe was a "tough kid," he thought, but maybe too tough. Her hard-shell exterior seemed to mask what he now knew was a difficult childhood.

During every service, attenders were provided with a time of silent prayer. Braedon bowed his head and immediately found himself thinking about the beautiful woman who sat across from him in the restaurant just twelve hours ago. Their conversation when he returned her to her place was also something that still had his head spinning. As he walked her to the door of her apartment, she turned to him saying, "I'd invite you in, but the place is a mess. That's what happens when I don't get my weekend to clean things up. But I suppose you at least want a kiss goodnight for having bought my dinner?" The whole thing was awkward, and he wasn't quite sure how to respond. All he could think of to say was that he was happy to have had the time to get to know her better and didn't expect anything in return.

But rather than allowing his mind to wander any further this morning, he began praying for her.

"Lord, I don't know what it is about Prudhoe Bonner, but I find myself wanting to know her better. I ask that you give her a safe and rewarding week on the job. I know you love her and want her to know you, but it doesn't appear she's paying much attention to you right now. In fact, I don't even know if she'll pay much attention to me either. Just give me the words to say to her, and keep my own will in check so that I reflect yours instead. Amen."

As he raised his head, the pastor was drawing the time to a close by praying aloud for the needs of the people. Before long, the benediction was spoken, and Braedon found himself back in his truck and on the way to his home on the outskirts of town. There he'd make lunch, mend a break in his fencing, and spend the rest of the day relaxing before what he anticipated to be a taxing workweek ahead.

The late sunsets this time of year always made it more difficult for Braedon to get to sleep at a reasonable time. This evening was no different as he lay on the couch with his malamute already asleep by the hearth. He was grateful for the friendly musher reject that he had named Bozo—after the world's most famous clown. After all, the dog was a clown with his occasional limp and funny eye markings on his mask and snout.

As Braedon was half dozing with the local newspaper over his face, the phone rang. Nearly coming out of his skin, he sat straight up and listened for a second ring before getting up to catch the call.

"Braedon here," he began.

"Braedon, it's Prudhoe. I hope I haven't caught you too late, but I wanted you to know I've had a chance to clean up around here and wondered if you'd like to come by my place. I've got cold beer in the refrigerator."

"Hello, Prudhoe, that's a great offer, but I'm afraid the timing isn't good. I've got an early phone call I need to take tomorrow morning from my new boss back in DC, and I have to be alert. I'd like a rain check, but maybe we should meet on neutral ground. After all, I have your reputation to consider."

There was a slight pause on the other end of the line, then laughter.

"Okay, big guy," Prudhoe chuckled. "I guess someone should be considering my reputation. Maybe another time. Hope you have a productive phone call tomorrow. Good-night."

"Goodnight, Prudhoe," he said soft and low before putting the receiver on the cradle.

CHAPTER 8

"Dika Nasak, if I didn't know better, I'd say this guy was playing hard to get," Prudhoe said, as she swirled the lukewarm coffee in the bottom of her cup.

"Look, I'm your friend, right? We've only got ten minutes of our meal period left, and I gotta have a smoke. Besides, even though this cafeteria is noisy, it still has ears. But we need to talk, so let's get together after our shift tonight. Meet me in the lobby near the emergency room," pleaded Dika.

"Okay, go smoke. See you then. So glad I gave up that habit years ago."

Prudhoe made her way back to her workstation and clocked back into work. Bothered by the fact that she'd not heard from Braedon Clarkson for more than a week now, she had begun to try to put a reason to the lack of communication. She was, after all, used to being in control and having men respond to her overtures on her terms.

Prudhoe thought she was the first to arrive in the lobby later that afternoon, until she caught a glimpse of Dika smoking just outside the doors. Walking out to the breezeway, she hooked her best friend's arm and started walking, forcing Dika to move with her.

"What a crappy day. Hope yours was better," commented Prudhoe, as Dika relented easily to being arm in arm with her friend of many years.

"Not bad. What made it so bad for you today?"

"Had to put on the lulusta today to cover for my sadness over a patient we lost this afternoon," responded Prudhoe.

As Dika kept looking straight ahead, she asked, "Lulusta?"

"Sorry—old language. It means mask in Bella Coola. I hate it when people die, especially the ones who aren't that old. This guy was just fifty-five years old. And you should know he died of lung cancer, so when are you gonna stop smoking anyway?"

"I don't have many vices, Prudhoe. Allow me this one. Besides, some of the docs say it helps with keeping weight off."

"Some trade off. Besides, you're not fat. Wouldn't you rather be healthy and hang on to your bad habit money?"

"Stop bugging me. Let's get back to the subject of this guy. What's his name again?"

"Braedon... Braedon Clarkson. Say, do you think it would be too brash of me to call him up and ask him out? After all, he asked me for the first date. Maybe it's my turn."

"No way, Prudhoe. Don't do it. Make him come to you. You're so pretty; he's probably thinking about you right now."

Prudhoe cleared her throat and threw Dika her best I-don't-believe-you look as the two made their way to the 515 bar. It went without saying that they'd end up there after work. And by the time they arrived, the place was crowded and smoke-filled. Given the female-to-male ratio in town, all eyes were on the two women as they entered and found one small table and two chairs open.

After more conversation about Braedon, Dika convinced Prudhoe not to make the next move. And before long, two guys pulled up chairs at the women's small table to buy the next round. They knew one of the men, but the other villager was new to them. Prudhoe was used to this tactic and often parlayed their obvious trick into some bar food as well.

By eight o'clock, it was time for the ladies to get home and prepare for the next work day. Saying their goodbyes, the two set off for the few blocks they walked together before going separate ways home. At least Dika had a husband to go home to, thought Prudhoe, as she walked along staring down at the sidewalk once they parted company.

It was still light enough for her to see some movement on her right side just past the tall hedges that stopped at a small alleyway. Thinking it was probably an animal, she wasn't the least bit concerned until she felt a strong hand grab her arm with a quick yank, and she was pulled through a thin part of the hedge. She felt each painful scrape of the exposed woody parts of the plant on her face until she found herself almost instantly on the other side and slammed hard onto the ground. The jagged rocks dug into her elbows, shoulders, and back. Before she could scream, another hand was over her mouth, and the face of a dark stranger was hovering over hers telling her to shut up.

"No screaming. No talking. No fighting. If you do, I'll kill you," he said in a low and scratchy whisper, the smell of alcohol on his breath.

She saw the flash of a switchblade out of the corner of her eye. Both panic and a split-second decision to comply came easily now. The fear of dying gripped her mind harder than the hands of the rapist now busy with his violent attack. Prudhoe went limp. Before passing out from the choke hold, she saw the first stars appearing in the evening sky and dark eagle wings cutting through the air overhead.

Waking to a half-moonlit night and a pounding headache, Prudhoe propped herself up on her elbows and found it difficult to catch her breath without effort. Her assailant was gone. She was alone. Along with pain came the shame; both rushed in upon her. Looking down, she could see one white shoe and torn white hosiery a few feet away. The small, black men's wallet that she carried in her uniform pocket was open by her side with the five-dollar bill missing.

Slowly sitting up, the tears leapt from her eyes as she considered that her only option was to return to the very emergency room she left a few hours earlier. Everyone knew her. If she reported the crime, everyone would know. People would whisper and avoid her.

As she gathered her shoe and put it back on, burning anger began to stir deep within her. She'd survived, but in her numb, limping walk back to the hospital, she vowed to never trust another man as long as she lived.

CHAPTER 9

The admitting clerk recognized her, yet simply stared as Prudhoe silently walked past her and through the double swinging interior doors of the emergency room. On the other side of those doors, Prudhoe flagged down the first available doctor she saw. The balding Doctor Poole had a reputation for being a very sincere soul with a great bedside manner. Prudhoe was grateful he was on duty.

She whispered, "I've just been raped, and this is the only place I know to come. Afraid to go home tonight, and I'm in pain. Can you help?"

The shocked look on his face told Prudhoe all she needed to know about how bad she must have looked.

"Of course, Nurse. Let me help you to room four. It's the farthest away from the entrance and the other patients we've got right now."

Over the next two hours, the police were called, and Dr. Poole had completed her examination. He determined that she'd sustained cuts, bruises and a small crack in the front lower rib. Additionally, she had a bruised tailbone and a sprained ankle. Though she knew she would recover from her physical injuries, the painful emotional ordeal was almost more than Prudhoe could cope with. However, she managed to accomplish the one thing she most wanted to do—give her statement and a description of her assailant to the police.

One of the nurses helped her shower and administered a painkiller and a sleep aid, all the while assuring Prudhoe that they'd keep her in emergency rather than admit her to a floor. For that, Prudhoe was grateful.

The nurse had kept her door shut for privacy, so Prudhoe awoke the next morning to her dark, windowless room. Though she had slept, she could sense that it was a fitful sleep. Her body ached all over, much like the feeling after being in a car wreck. She knew that feeling because she'd been in one of those many years ago with her mother at the wheel after having too much to drink. They had both been fortunate to walk away with minor cuts and bruises.

Prudhoe thought about using the call button to get help using the bathroom. Then she realized another shift with a different nurse would be on duty this morning. No sooner had the dread of having to face someone else come upon her than she saw light gleaming from around the door as it opened slowly.

"Prudy, it's me, Dika," said the whispering shadow.

"Oh, Dika, I'm so glad to see you. Do you...," Prudhoe stopped herself.

"Know? Yes, I told you these hospital walls have ears. The night shift nurse called me because she knows we're friends. She just figured since you don't have family here... "

"Sure. I understand," Prudhoe said in a low voice, as Dika shut the door. The moment she did, Prudhoe broke down crying, and Dika ran to her bedside. She pulled the chain on the small florescent light fixture above the bed so they might have a bit of light.

"Oh, Prudy, this is awful, but we'll get through it. The most important thing is that you get well and strong again. I feel terrible that this happened after we went our separate ways last night."

Through her tears, Prudhoe told Dika what had happened the night before. She also wanted her friend to know that she couldn't have known and shouldn't bear any guilt for simply going home. Dika laid her head next to Prudhoe's head and asked her what she could do for her.

"Well, if you don't mind, can you help me get up to go to the bathroom? Given the sprained ankle, I'll probably need a wheelchair so I don't put my weight on it."

Dika scurried out of the room to grab a wheelchair, making sure to close the door behind her. It left Prudhoe alone again...and this time she panicked. She could feel the hair on the back of her neck rise and her breath shorten. She tried hard to get a grip on her emotions, reminding herself that fear, anger, and sadness were going to be a part of any journey to recovery she'd witnessed as a nurse. As she lay there in the dimly lit room, it all seemed so overwhelming. She'd always felt like she was strong enough to endure anything, but now she found herself questioning her resiliency.

Finally, Dika returned and helped her off the bed and into the wheelchair.

"You know, the shift nurse saw me and reminded me that I'm not supposed to be providing care," said Dika.

"Well, I hope you told her to shove it," remarked Prudhoe out of frustration and pain.

"No, I did not, silly. She's bigger than me!"

After Dika got Prudhoe to the bathroom and back to the bed, the shift nurse showed up, and Dika excused herself to go home to put on her uniform and report for duty upstairs.

Before leaving, she kissed Prudhoe on the forehead and told her she'd see her soon.

Chapter 10

Prudhoe was glad to be home and relieved that Dika had agreed to stay with her for the next several days. It gave her someone else to focus on and talk to. However, her emotions ran wild at night, making it difficult to get to sleep. Sometimes she'd lie awake for hours.

On the evening of the third day after Prudhoe's discharge, the phone rang while she and Dika were eating a light dinner together and watching television. Since Dika insisted that Prudhoe not move around much given her bandaged rib cage and bad ankle, she was the one to answer the phone.

Prudhoe could overhear Dika say, "Hello. Yes, she's here. This is her friend Dika. Can I tell her who is calling? Oh... ah... sure, let me get her."

Holding her hand over the receiver, Dika whispered, "It's that guy... Braedon. What do you say?"

"I say I don't want to talk to him. In fact, I don't care if I ever see him again," Prudhoe answered with a huff.

"Prudy, you can't treat everyone like that. He can't be held responsible for what you just went through. He doesn't know what happened."

"I know, but tell him to call back tomorrow when I'm feeling better. I'm not ready."

Lifting her hand off the receiver, Dika indicated that Prudhoe hadn't been feeling well and asked if he might call her back tomorrow. After hanging up, she returned to the couch with Prudhoe.

"Okay, I told him, but you're just putting off the inevitable."

"I suppose you're right, but I just want to hide, Dika. In fact, I can't even think about returning to work in a few weeks, though I know I'll have to. Tomorrow I have to call my supervisor and give her an update on my progress. It feels so strange talking to people about my condition like it's just the flu or something. I don't know what they know, and I'm too ashamed to talk about it."

"Oh, sweetie, I'm only able to sympathize, having never been through such trauma, so I can't know what you must be going through. I'm so sorry."

"Just don't pity me, Dika. I hate that."

"I don't pity you, Prudhoe. I know you will get through this. You will never forget the attack, but it will fade as the years pass. That's what has happened to me over the miscarriage I had four years ago. I wish I had a child to replace that one, but I guess it's just not meant to be. I'll never forget, but the pain softens with time."

"I'm sorry, Dika. I didn't mean to be so short with you. I am bouncing back and forth between feeling sorry for myself and trying to regain my footing. And it's hard to accept that some of the most difficult things are still ahead of me. Things like returning to work, having people stare at me and talk behind my back, having to return for a check back with the doc in ten days, and also having to face the police again to look at photos of suspects. I just want to go to sleep and wake up in a world where none of this happened."

"I know. Through it all, I'll be here for you. Patuk is doing fine by himself, and he's glad you have my company. He knows I'll be back home to clean up after him pretty soon. See, I probably couldn't handle having a kid anyway because my own husband is enough to keep after!"

For the first time since the attack, Prudhoe smiled at her friend.

CHAPTER 11

The phone rang in the early afternoon when Prudhoe was alone. It rang several times before she got to it, mostly because she took a few seconds to decide whether or not to answer it at all.

"Hello."

"Prudhoe, this is Braedon. I was sorry to hear you've been under the weather. Is there anything I can do or bring you?"

"No... no, I'll be fine."

"You don't sound fine, but I won't intrude. I just wanted to know if I might feed you another chicken dinner again this weekend."

Prudhoe considered responding with the simple question of *why*, but thought better of it.

"Sure, as long as that weekend is not this one. I'll probably be well enough to go to dinner in about two weeks."

"Two weeks? You really are in a bad way. Are you sure there isn't something I can do for you?"

"I'm sure. I'll be fine. Let's talk again in a few weeks, if you're still interested."

"Interested? Prudhoe, I remain interested in getting to know you better. I hope you'll let me. I'll call back next week to check in on you. Meanwhile, I'll be praying for your recovery from whatever ails you."

"You do that. Goodnight, Braedon."

After hanging up the phone, Prudhoe felt like throwing it across the room. Even though she knew Braedon wasn't the one she was angry with, his call reminded her of her distrust of men, which was exacerbated by what had happened to her last week. She also realized she was angry that he had something she didn't have... faith. She wasn't sure what he put his faith in, or even if it was something worth putting his faith in. She just knew that he seemed to have an inner strength and peace that she wished she had.

Once Dika returned to her husband and household, Prudhoe felt the loss. She kept the television or radio on all day just to hear human voices. It was somewhat comforting and also served as a distraction from her emotional pain. By the end of the week, she welcomed Braedon's "just checking in" phone call. After all, he had that prayer thing—someone he could talk to, thought Prudhoe. She didn't have anyone to talk to. This time they talked for several minutes, and he even got her to chuckle over a funny joke his coworker had told him that day. The call came at a great time because tomorrow she was going to the doctor for tests and another exam. She couldn't tell Braedon about her dread, so tonight she pretended she was doing fine. In fact, she wasn't sure she could ever tell him... or trust him.

As the week progressed, Prudhoe's cuts and bruises were healing. She'd received negative test results for certain sexually transmitted diseases and pregnancy. She stopped wearing a scarf around her neck when she went to the grocery or drug store. It had been there to cover the thumbprint bruise under her left ear from the choke hold she'd been in.

Even with the good news of healing, she was still angry, scared, and depressed. She hadn't even contacted her mother and had decided it was a secret she'd keep from her anyway. After all, her mother had troubles enough of her own and would probably just ask for money again. Bella Bonner had never remarried after Prudhoe's dad had abandoned them. She lived in Juneau and worked for a fish processing company. Prudhoe hadn't seen her mother for nearly a year, and she also didn't think her first contact should be about this terrible event.

CHAPTER 12

Prudhoe was slated to return to work on Sunday, albeit to limited duty with respect to lifting. She was looking forward to being able to focus on helping others—the reason she got into nursing in the first place. But before returning to work, she'd agreed to meet Braedon at the restaurant again for dinner on Saturday night. She had showered and put on her best dress for the dinner. Prudhoe loved the sleeveless, floral-patterned dress in red, a color that looked good on her. She generally went for bright colors because she tired of wearing a plain uniform most of the time. And though the weather in June could sometimes be cooperative in Anchorage, she still threw a light blue shawl wrap over the dress.

Rather than have Braedon pick her up, she drove herself. Patuk had made some repairs to her truck, and driving her own vehicle always made her feel independent. Frankly, she also liked the ability to part company whenever she wanted to, and the need to control her circumstances was even stronger these days.

As she grabbed her handbag off the passenger seat and slipped out of the truck, she saw Braedon getting out of his truck on the other side of the parking lot. As the two made their way toward the front door of the restaurant, he made eye contact and waved at her. Arriving at the door before her, he held it for her while saying, "My goodness, if you've been ill, no one would ever know it. You look lovely this evening, Prudhoe." She mustered a quiet "thanks" as she walked inside.

Secreted away at a back table, the couple spent the next two hours talking. Braedon had Prudhoe talking about her ancestry as far back as the oral history had been passed down to her. She told him about her mother as well as her grandmother, who was born in the late 1800s, had married a Nuxalk, and then moved from British Columbia to Alaska when widowed. They even talked about her great-grandmother, who lived in the Bella Coola Valley until her husband died of smallpox. The great-grandmother came up when Braedon asked about the simple copper bracelet that Prudhoe wore on her wrist.

"It was handed down to me through my mom from my great-great-great-grandmother, who died during childbirth, leaving my great-great-grandmother to be raised by her father for the first fifteen years of her life before he died and left her on her own. My people believe that everything belongs to those not yet born, so preserving something for the future generation was important. The bracelet is like a long string that is held on the other end by its maker, said to have been a Nuxalk in the sixteenth century. We are held together across time by that string."

"Prudhoe, that's an amazing story. Your past is much more interesting than mine," commented Braedon. "Tell me how you got your name."

"I was born in 1930 in Fairbanks, where my father barely worked, but we moved to Anchorage when I was three. I guess my parents liked the name of Prudhoe Bay up north and wanted me to remain in Alaska when I got older. How did you get yours?"

"Hmm, the name isn't even a family name. I think my mom just liked the name, and my dad deferred to her. My folks, Jack and Joanne Clarkson, live over in Thane, but I was born in Juneau in 1927. Our family history in Alaska starts with my great-grandfather homesteading from Illinois. He came by boat at the turn of the century during the gold rush and mined with the Jack Wade Mining District northeast of Fairbanks. By 1915, he landed work as a miner in the Juneau area but eventually went back to farming and filed for a homestead near Thane. The old sourdough finally got his title to the sixty acres a few months before his seventy-third birthday. Even as much as I think I have some pretty good survival skills, I am in awe of his having packed up everything to live on a plot accessible only by train and building his house from scratch in this inhospitable territory."

"Your family history is just as interesting as mine, Braedon. That's fascinating."

Just as she finished her sentence, Braedon reached across the table, past their empty plates, to put his hand on hers. Prudhoe immediately withdrew her hand from the table before realizing how her action might be seen as rejection.

"I'm sorry...just jumpy, I guess."

"I don't understand. Do I make you uncomfortable?" asked Braedon.

"No, you have always been kind to me. I am just feeling unsure of things right now."

"Is there anything you want to tell me, Prudhoe?"

"I don't think I can. It's just that you don't really know me, and I don't really know you. I feel like I can talk to you with ease, but I am not very trusting."

"You've been hurt in your past. That much I know. I also know that we'll never get to know one another if you believe you can't talk to me... or trust me. I want you to know that I will hide your deepest secrets as though they were my own. I can't make you trust me, but I hope you'll come to find me trustworthy."

"How do I know you aren't simply after the one thing all men are after?" Prudhoe blurted out, before remembering they were in a public place. She looked over her shoulder then back at Braedon, who registered a genuine look of concern.

"Prudhoe, let's get out of here and go someplace where we can talk privately," suggested Braedon.

As they left the restaurant, Braedon grabbed Prudhoe's hand and walked her to his truck.

"Look, I'll drive us to the local park where we can take a walk and talk."

"No, please, not outside," Prudhoe pleaded.

"Well, we can't go to your place or mine. I told you once that I have your reputation to consider, so I'm not going to have you be seen going to into my home with me alone. I won't walk into your place alone with you either. I'll tell you what, let's just get in the truck, and we'll drive to the parking lot of the library. We can sit in the truck without being interrupted because the library is closed now. Would that be okay?"

Prudhoe agreed and got in the truck while he held the door for her. Driving a few miles, Braedon pulled into the library driveway and parked. Turning toward Prudhoe and leaning up against the driver's side door, he sat quietly for a few minutes before he spoke.

"You've been in my thoughts and prayers, Prudhoe."

Prudhoe felt the lump in her throat and tears beginning to rim her eyes as she turned her head toward the passenger side window. The fear, sadness, and anger came rushing back to her.

"Yeah, well, your God was nowhere to be found a few weeks ago when I coulda used his help," she said in a loud voice as she turned to face Braedon.

"Do you want to tell me about it?"

"Not really. I'll get through this too," she responded.

"Does this have anything to do with your falling ill?"

In defiance, she blurted out, "I didn't fall ill. I was raped walking home after work. There—now you know."

Braedon swallowed hard but kept his eyes on Prudhoe.

"God isn't the author of sin, Prudhoe. Don't blame him for the evil deeds of men. And you aren't to blame for this evil deed either. No one deserves to be violated. I am so sorry this has happened to you. If you'll let me in, I'll prove to you that God loves you. . . and that I care about you very much."

CHAPTER 13

The alarm clock slammed against Prudhoe's deep sleep the next morning. Being a bit too used to getting up late over the last several weeks, she covered her head with the sheets, desperately wanting to turn the thing off and go back to sleep. After all, this wasn't going to be an easy day. First, there would be the awkward comments from staff who did know. Then there would be the inevitable questions from those who didn't know. And to make it worse, she had to use her lunchtime to go to the police department to review photos of potential perpetrators again.

Pulling the covers off her head, she reached over to turn off the alarm and slowly began the process of getting herself ready. One of the only things that made her happy was the updated new uniform that Dika and Patuk had bought for her so she could trash the one she was wearing that horrible night. Prudhoe was so grateful for it, especially because she knew that Dika had to sacrifice to buy it. Prudhoe was determined to find a way to pay Dika back for her kindness.

As she got in the shower after having some coffee, her mind returned to last night's discussion in the cab of Braedon's truck. She thought about how sensitive he'd been toward her situation. Then she reflected on his plea that she consider what he had to say about a God who was above all others... and that this God loved her. It shook her to the core when Braedon spoke about how this God had sent his son into the world to live a perfect life and then lay down his life for mankind to be reconciled to God. He said it was a substitutionary act because people aren't perfect. And while it made some sense to her, she still thought that perhaps she might have to clean up her act before she could approach such a God.

She'd given Braedon her word that she'd remain open to hearing more. However, she still wondered about his intentions relative to her. Was he some kind of preacher who simply wanted to cut another notch in his "salvation" belt? Did he really mean it when he said he cared about her, or was he just taking pity on her? So many questions filled her mind, but at least they pushed out the thoughts of going to work.

The last thing she'd done on her way home the night before was put gas in her truck. No more walking to and from work anymore, of that she was sure. Besides, she'd need it to drive to the police station today.

As she made the short drive to the hospital and parked, her self-confidence was in retreat. She sat in the truck and took several deep breaths before heading inside to work. She avoided taking the elevator and instead chose to take the stairs, all the while realizing that eventually she was going to have to face people again. And sure enough, the minute she popped out of the stairwell she almost ran into the charge nurse.

"Oh, sorry, Prudhoe, not used to having someone come out of that door. I saw your name on the schedule for this morning, but I don't think we have a release from the doctor. Are you able to return to full duty?"

"I have a written release in my wallet for you. I can work, but no unassisted lifting this week for me. Want me to leave the note at the station?"

Her supervisor nodded affirmatively and appeared to want to say something. Instead, she sighed heavily and started toward one of the patient rooms. After a few steps, she stopped and turned back to Prudhoe saying, "I'm so sorry, dear. Let me know if there's anything I can do."

Prudhoe did her best to smile and then headed to the nurses station to check in and look over the census. At this point, she was almost relieved that she would spend her lunchtime with the police instead of in the hospital lunchroom. Even as she took on each task in her rounds, she was already feeling increasingly anxious about having to be at the police station that afternoon.

She took some solace in knowing that at least it wasn't going to be a lineup she'd have to look at—just photos. Furthermore, the police had already told her that they had reason to believe a failed attack of a similar nature had happened about four weeks earlier on the other side of town. They had a pretty good description from that victim, and it matched most of the details Prudhoe had given them. Prudhoe was glad to hear the other woman had escaped and didn't endure what she'd been through. She was also encouraged that perhaps the assailant would be quickly identified, punished, and taken off the streets.

By lunchtime Prudhoe was feeling a bit stronger. That is, until the detective dropped the book of mug shots in front of her on the desk at the police station. She felt the thud through her knee, which was up against the desk. A knot developed in her stomach. And even though she had a sense that the face of her attacker wouldn't be found in the book, when she opened it to the first page, she drew in a small breath upon seeing his entry at the bottom.

Prudhoe was instantly taken back to the leathery-skinned figure in the shadows. His eyes looked dead in the head shot, and she saw the scar under his left ear in the profile photo. Her hatred for him must have been evident in her flashing eyes because the detective asked her to put her finger on the correct photo. It was almost too much to ask. Prudhoe felt like her index finger would burn as hot as her anger if she touched the picture, but she complied.

Chapter 14

Upon arriving home after her first day back at work, Prudhoe was in her small kitchen preparing herself some dinner when the phone rang. It was the detective she'd met with earlier that day. He wanted her to know that the other victim had identified the same man from the photo file, and they had picked up the Yupik male on some lesser charge of temporary appropriation of a vehicle. She was relieved to know he was in custody now and that the detectives would develop the rape and attempted rape charges for the prosecutor's office. What she wasn't looking forward to was being a primary witness at the hearing.

Soon after Prudhoe had settled into her bathrobe in front of the television, the phone rang again. This time it was Bracdon.

"Hello, Prudhoe. I am checking in to see how your first day back to work went. Based on our conversation last night, I knew you were dreading it."

"Thanks for thinking of me. I'd say it went about as well as one could expect. My coworkers just didn't know what to say. Frankly, I didn't know what to say either, so I just focused on my patients."

"I know you also had to review the police photos today. Any progress there?"

"Yes, I saw that hideous face. I hate him. But the good news is that the police called tonight to tell me they had picked him up and put him in jail. I hope he rots, but not until he's charged and found guilty. I just don't want to have to be in the courtroom... or anywhere near him."

Braedon detected her voice cracking and didn't want to further upset her with the painful memory.

"I can imagine you don't. Listen, Prudhoe, I want you to feel free to call me anytime you need someone to talk to. Remember, I'm a friend, so I want to help you heal from this devastating event."

"Well, I'll try not to bother you, but I appreciate the offer. According to my friend Dika, it's a grieving process. It certainly feels like it."

"You aren't bothering me. You've got to realize that grief is a form of validation; it says the wound matters. You matter. This isn't the way things are supposed to be, so your friend is right. She sounds like a good friend, and I'm glad you have her. Just know that you have me too."

"Thanks. And thanks for calling. I hope you have a good evening."

"You take care of yourself. I'll check in with you later this week, if that's okay with you."

As they said their goodbyes and Prudhoe hung up the phone, she felt so many mixed emotions. She was glad to have Braedon to lean on; he seemed so wise and strong. On the other hand, she still wasn't sure she could trust him... or anyone. After all, maybe he just felt sorry for her. Or maybe he just wanted sex. And if the latter, could it be because he saw her as "damaged goods" anyway? On the other hand... Oh, enough of this, she thought as she shook her head and plopped back down on the couch where she eventually fell asleep.

The next morning came quickly. Still on the couch and without her alarm clock, Prudhoe panicked when she awoke. Checking the clock on her stove, she realized there was no time for coffee this morning. Showering and prepping for work was all she'd have time for.

Arriving just one minute before the start of her shift wasn't her habit, and her supervisor noted it by asking her if she was all right.

"Sure thing... Just fell asleep on the couch without my alarm. Good thing my body seems to know when it's time to go to work," she responded without emotion. In fact, hearing her own tone of voice made her wonder if she ever wanted to feel emotions again. She just wanted to feel strong again.

Chapter 15

As the summer passed, it wasn't long before things seemed to slip back into a routine for Prudhoe. The only thing missing was her social life at the bar, but she really wasn't that interested anymore because the prosecutor had informed her that the defendant may have been seen in the bar earlier on the night of the assault. Now she knew he had followed her and Dika and made his move when she went her own way. She didn't tell Dika that detail because she didn't want her friend to feel any more guilt than she already had expressed for not being with Prudhoe that night. And while she was grateful that he hadn't hurt Dika, it didn't lessen the pain and shame she felt. And much of that was going to have to be revisited because a trial date had been set for late September, now just a few weeks away.

The highlights of the summer had been the times that she and Braedon had spent together. He had even taken her north to Palmer for the fun and food of the Alaska State Fair. Always the gentleman and always in public places, he held her hand, listened, and consoled. She was looking forward to seeing him again this Saturday when they'd agreed to do some hiking in the Chugach National Forest. It was just a few days away now, and she was looking forward to spending time with him on the trails. Prudhoe was feeling stronger and thought it might even be a way of testing him. After all his talk about being a Christian, she still figured he was a red-blooded male who couldn't possibly be as strong of will as she was. She was sure to find out that he was just like all the others.

When Saturday arrived, Braedon picked her up in his truck, which held two backpacks containing first aid items, food, and water for the two of them. As they drove along the scenic Seward Highway, they talked about how fortunate they were to have a rare sunny day this far into September. At least they could use the sunny areas to warm from the forty-degree high temperature that was forecasted on the radio. It was also an opportunity for Prudhoe to tell Braedon that she'd achieved enough seniority to put in for a change to day shift, Mondays through Fridays, and would be starting on that new schedule the following week.

"Great news, Prudhoe," said Braedon with clear excitement in his voice. "What made you decide to do that?"

"I've wanted that schedule for quite some time but knew it would have to come in stages. Everyone wants weekdays and day shift hours, but it takes a while to get there. Most nurses start on nights, or even part-time, and work toward whatever works best for their circumstances. I guess I just wanted to have my weekend when most people have theirs."

"Well, I must confess to being very happy that you're joining me in that schedule. Perhaps you'd be willing to spend your first available Sunday with me at my church service?" Braedon speculated out loud.

"Uh, I dunno about that. You know I'm not much of a church-type person. I'd feel pretty sheepish about that. I might need some time to get my act together before facing your God."

Braedon chuckled as he drove and then glanced over at the beautiful woman on the other side of the bench seat.

"Prudhoe, sheepish is exactly how he wants us to come. He's the Great Shepherd, after all! Besides, you don't come to him after you get your act together or in your own strength. You simply come as you are, and he'll be your strength from then on."

"Yeah, well, give me some time to think about that. It's not that I don't enjoy your company. You've been a swell guy and all. Let's just say that I'm probably not ready for that yet."

Braedon kept driving and didn't say another word until they reached the trailhead, where he parked the truck. As they put on their backpacks and started off, he assured her that he knew the park well but she should let him know if she was getting tired or needed to stop along the way. Prudhoe knew her guide was an expert, and the rifle he slung over his shoulder was also comforting given some of the dangerous wild animals in Alaska.

As they took in the breathtaking scenery for several hours, they talked about their jobs, their aspirations, family, and friends. Despite herself, Prudhoe realized that she was starting to become close to Braedon. So much so that Dika had referred to them as "inseparable" these days. Not that Dika was upset with the growing relationship between Prudhoe and Braedon. In fact, Prudhoe secretly suspected that Dika was hoping it might eventually lead to something. As independent as Prudhoe was, Dika knew that her best friend longed for companionship that went deeper than the one-night stands and occasional short-term relationships that Prudhoe had pursued in the past. Dika had even confronted Prudhoe once about whether or not she was afraid of commitment because of her distrust of men. Prudhoe denied it, but she never forgot the question Dika raised that day.

Around noon, the two hikers stopped by the river to lay out the small tarp that Braedon had packed. They'd pulled out their lunch and continued their conversation, thoroughly enjoying each other's company. After they had eaten and stored things back in their packs, they continued to enjoy the sunny spot they had chosen.

"Did you see the termination dust on the Chugach?" Braedon asked.

"Sure did. I noticed the first snow cover this past week. Our summers are so short, and I feel a serious winter coming on," Prudhoe responded.

"Oh yeah? Is that something you heard, or are you drawing on your native instincts for that information?" he asked.

"Okay, no special native insight here. I just know we always have hard winters. It's a pretty safe prediction, don't you think?"

Braedon turned toward Prudhoe just as she leaned in toward him. Without any hesitation, he kissed her rosebud lips. Prudhoe felt the electricity in the kiss, but Braedon stopped and quickly faced forward and leaned back.

"What's the matter? Didn't you like that?" she asked.

"I did like that. In fact, I liked it very much," he answered.

"You're blushing!" Prudhoe exclaimed.

"I suppose I am. I should apologize. I took that opportunity, rather than asking if you were okay with it."

"I'm fine with it...more than fine. In fact, since we haven't seen any other hikers for the last two hours, maybe we should try some more of that."

"Prudhoe, I am not going to take advantage of you. I'd never do that. I couldn't. And I don't mean that just because of what you've been through. I mean that I want our relationship to be built on more than a simple physical attraction. Don't get me wrong, I am very attracted to you, but we're still getting to know each other. And though I admit that I have strong feelings for you, we must take it slow," Braedon explained.

"Okay. I guess you're a fall in love first and then have sex kinda guy then?" Prudhoe asked with a wink.

"No, I'm a fall in love, get married, and then have sex kind of guy."

"Even without marriage, love and sex go together, Braedon. Is this some kind of religious hang-up you've got going?"

"My choices are faith-based, Prudhoe, and they're based on the knowledge that sex and love aren't the same thing. I'm sure sex is great, but love is something special—a patient commitment to care for the heart of the one you walk with for life."

"Yeah, I've heard about that kind of thing, but I'm not sure it really exists. I think sex binds two hearts together in love," Prudhoe blurted out in a near-defiant tone.

"Let me ask you, Prudhoe, was sex equivalent to love when you were attacked last spring?"

Prudhoe's ire was up before, but now it burned red hot. She turned to face Braedon and raised her hand to slap him across the face. His quick reflexes caught her wrist in midswing, and he pulled her to his big chest. Prudhoe found herself sobbing uncontrollably as he held her and stroked her long hair.

"I'm sorry. I shouldn't have brought that up. You and I both know that wasn't love. It was violent aggression and control. I only want you to understand that sex outside of marital commitment is just two people living for themselves. It's based on a feeling rather than a decision."

They sat in silence, wrapped up in each other for nearly twenty minutes. At the end of that time, Braedon looked down to see his precious but overwrought beauty had fallen asleep. It was gratifying for him to know she felt safe enough to finally let down her guard with him.

CHAPTER 16

The courthouse was cold that day because the heating systems were down and being worked on by city maintenance employees. Prudhoe already felt the chill in her bones as she walked through the double glass doors to see her assigned attorney waiting for her outside the courtroom. She'd followed all his instructions during their preparatory meetings the week prior to this day. She wore a conservative brown wool suit and low heels and put her hair up. She'd also steeled herself for the cross-examination grilling he told her she'd receive.

"Good morning, Miss Bonner," the prosecutor said. He reached out to shake her hand as she was removing her gloves. Prudhoe noticed the deep wrinkles on the weary face of the white-haired man.

"Hello, Mr. Shaw. I'm not convinced it's a good morning, but I'm ready to get this over with."

"Good. I know this is going to be difficult, Miss Bonner, but try to relax. Let me show you to our sidebar room."

They walked down the hall, and Shaw showed her into a small windowless room, where another man sat with his notebook open and pen flying quickly across the page.

"Miss Bonner, I want you to meet my assistant, Mr. Brooks. He's going to be helping both of us. He'll see to your needs and also keep me on track during the hearing."

Prudhoe reached across the small gray metal table to shake the younger attorney's hand as he stood in her presence. His crew cut and muscular physique made him look more like a military recruit. The three took their seats, each occupying a side of the rectangular table.

"Miss Bonner," Shaw began. "I've had several conversations with the defense attorney. As I told you last week, I suspected he'd be interested in pleading down the charges. The first sign of that was the defendant's waiver of a jury trial. I know you said that bargaining was unacceptable to you, but I thought I'd ask again because I'm pretty sure they know their case is weak. They are left with the assailant's claim that he was at home with his mother at the time of the attack, but his mother is a lousy witness for his alibi, given her history of alcoholism and documented onset of dementia."

"No. I'm still not interested, Mr. Shaw. I want this guy behind bars for a long time so he can't hurt anyone else. And because I hate him," responded Prudhoe with a cold and expressionless face.

"Very well, we'll proceed. We should probably get to the courtroom. Remember to stand when the judge is announced in the courtroom—even if Mr. Brooks has to help you up."

"I won't need any help," snapped Prudhoe.

The three proceeded out of the small room and into the musty hallway toward the courtroom door. Brooks held the door for Prudhoe and Shaw. As she entered behind the prosecutor, she could see the defendant's back as he sat in a chair with his assigned attorney just past the railing on the right. She felt the hair on the back of her neck lift. He was wearing street clothes with some kind of vest that looked more like the dirty gray lining zipped out of a parka.

As she looked to her left and kept walking toward the swinging door at the center of the railing, she spotted Braedon in the second row. He had indicated he'd be there for her, despite her pleas for him not to come. It warmed her heart to have Braedon there to support her, but she hated the thought of him having to hear the gritty details of the crime committed against her.

Arriving at the table beyond the railing, Shaw and Brooks sat on either side of her. As she took her seat she felt hemmed in and stiff. The only movement she made was to rub her hands up and down her cold arms twice. She dropped her hands to her lap and stared straight ahead while noticing in her peripheral vision that Shaw had turned to reach for something behind her. He proceeded to put a man's suit jacket around her shoulders. It was still warm, and she immediately recognized the scent of Braedon's aftershave on it.

Tears of gratitude mixed with fear were mounting when the bailiff stood at attention, saying, "All rise. The Honorable Judge Darin Hall presiding." Her tears stopped in their tracks as she stood and watched the black-robed judge take his seat at his raised desk before requesting everyone to be seated. Soon after, he was summoning the lead attorneys to approach the bench, and things got underway.

There were several things that Prudhoe felt prepared for, such as her own testimony and that of the attending physician in her case. But during a brief whispering session in advance of being called first to the stand, she saw the witness list in front of her attorney. Dika's name was on the list of both her attorney and that of the defendant. Even more confusing than that was the information Shaw imparted to her that the victim of attempted rape by the same man had chosen not to press charges.

"What? Why would she let him get away with this?" she inquired of Shaw with her best attempt to keep her voice hushed.

"I can't answer for her, Prudhoe, but I will tell you that she's Yupik herself. Perhaps that had something to do with it," he whispered in her ear.

The thought of potential tribal protectionism stirred even more anger and indignation in Prudhoe. Even though her attorney mentioned that he had won the right to provide the initial police report of the other woman's assault into evidence with the judge, it was little consolation. She felt as though she had to carry the weight of the entire trial on her word against that of her rapist. And why would his attorney want Dika on the witness stand? It was all so confusing and painful, though she would once again wear her mask and do what needed to be done.

Leaving Braedon's jacket in her chair, Prudhoe walked to the stand and took the oath before being seated. Shaw stood and began the process of drawing out her detailed account of that horrible night. She still couldn't look at the accused but instead kept her eyes on Shaw as she steadily and methodically answered his questions. Only once did the judge ask a question before cross-examination started, having her describe the switchblade she saw that night. Prudhoe relived her fear of being killed as she described the knife length and type and seeing the flash of silver in the handle as it caught the moonlight on the night of the attack.

Prudhoe was repulsed by the rapist's attorney. He was bulbous, pasty-skinned, and looked like a pugilist who had his nose broken one too many times. Furthermore, his lilting nasal voice didn't fit his body type.

Leaning on the rail of the stand he opened with, "Miss Bonner, you are unmarried, correct?"

"Yes."

"But not unattached apparently. Isn't that gentleman in the second row your current boyfriend?"

"Objection!" shouted her attorney as he bolted out of his chair.

"Sustained," declared the judge in a very matter-of-fact tone.

"Very well, Miss Bonner, can you tell me how often you frequented the 515 bar on say, a monthly basis?"

Prudhoe took a deep breath and slowly responded, "Weekly." She was now resigned to a very long and difficult morning.

CHAPTER 17

Prudhoe's emergency room physician arrived after the mid-morning break. He was promptly called to the stand and proceeded to detail her injuries, which were consistent with rape, as well as medical testing results. Cross-examination was limited largely to questions about the doctor being employed at the same hospital where Prudhoe worked.

After lunch break, Dika was called to the stand. She was ushered into the courtroom and walked through the swinging door of the railing toward the stand and was sworn in. She explained her longtime friendship with "Prudy" and what occurred on the night in question under gentle questioning from Shaw. It was the cross-examination that was difficult for Prudhoe to watch. Dika shifted in her chair as the rapist's attorney asked about how many drinks they had, who they sat with, and how often they frequented the bar. But the most stunning response came when the attorney asked if she'd ever seen the defendant before.

"Yes."

"Can you tell us where and when you've seen him, please?"

"I've seen him in the hospital visiting his mother when she was admitted with pneumonia."

"How often did he visit his mother there?"

"Every day for ten days."

"Thank you. That will be all."

Prudhoe could certainly see the setup in the portrayal of her attacker as a poor but loyal son, devoted to his mother and therefore incapable of a horrendous crime.

By late afternoon, the defendant was called to the stand by his own attorney. Though he took an oath to tell the truth, he claimed innocence of the crime. He told the court that he'd never seen Prudhoe before the trial, and that he'd been at his mother's home on the date and at the time of the attack.

When the judge called on Shaw for cross-examination, he only had one question. He asked the defendant to confirm his ownership of the switchblade entered into exhibit, to which the pudgy attorney objected, suggesting that lots of men carry knives on their person. The judge sustained the objection.

Shaw declined further questioning and indicated that he had read the statement on the record made by the defendant's mother that appeared to corroborate his alibi. He did ask the judge to carefully review the mother's medical records, also provided to the court. Shaw then indicated to the judge that he had one more witness to call to the stand, though his name hadn't appeared on the original list. The defense attorney objected, and the judge called them both to his bench. Once the threesome ended their conversation, the judge indicated that Shaw could call William J. Banks to the stand.

Prudhoe was completely baffled by this turn of events, but even more so when she saw her favorite bartender walking past her to take the stand. Billy's tall and lanky frame was hard to mistake, even under his oversized jacket.

"Mr. Banks," began Shaw, Do you typically go by Billy?"

"Yep, Billy is fine."

"Can you tell the court if you've ever seen the defendant in your bar, the 515?"

"Sure can. I seen him there, but just once. It was on the same night that Miss Bonner was attacked. It was that man sitting right there," responded Billy as he pointed to the defendant.

"Would that be before the confirmed time of the attack, during that time, or after the attack?"

"It was before the attack, when Miss Bonner and her friends were at the bar that night. In fact, he'd already been there for about an hour before Prudhoe and Dika walked in the door."

"What was he doing—or was there anything different about this patron?"

"He was drinking. That's what folks do in the bar. But I did notice that he kept looking over at the two women. I watch my female patrons pretty closely, and he seemed to take a big interest in them."

"Did you notice anything else, Billy?"

"Yep, when the gals were gathering up their things and paying their tab, he didn't finish his half-full glass and quickly dropped cash on the bar for me, as well as a switchblade that fell out while he was fumbling for the money."

Holding up a clear plastic bag, Shaw asked, "Billy, here is a switchblade obtained from the defendant at the time of his arrest. Can you identify it as the kind you saw dropped on the bar that night?"

As Billy looked over the blade, he nodded affirmatively, but Shaw asked him to confirm verbally for the court record.

"Yep, looks like the same blade I saw that night, down to the diamond-shaped silver inset on the handle."

"Did the man you see before you today manage to leave before the two women left?"

"Sure did, after picking up his blade and putting it back in his pocket. He didn't even wait for change."

When the judge asked the defense attorney if he wanted to cross-examine the witness, he declined.

CHAPTER 18

Prudhoe was back on the job again on Monday. Judge Hall had brought things to a close at five o'clock the previous Friday by setting a date for his ruling on the verdict one week hence. She just wanted to get through this week, her first one in the new schedule of Monday through Friday. But the days seemed to crawl by, made worse by the low census on her floor that week. She'd have to appear back in court on Friday morning but wasn't expected to return to work that day.

She'd heard from Braedon, who made sure to call her regularly during this difficult time. He was consistent in his friendship, though Prudhoe wondered if that might change once this ordeal was over. In fact, in one of those phone calls that came midweek, she tested those waters.

"So, I suppose once this is over you'll stop hovering over me?"

"Do you want less attention from me, Prudhoe?" he asked.

"I'm not saying that; I just figured you were being extra nice to me right now. I don't want you to feel obligated to take care of me. I'm going to be fine. I always have been."

"Will you always be pushing me away in your distrust? How can I break through your tough exterior to make you understand that I genuinely care about you?"

"I suppose you could take me out to a nice dinner on the town when this is all over," Prudhoe said in an almost dismissive tone.

"I'll take you to a nice lunch on Sunday, but only after you attend my church service with me. How's that for a bribe?"

"Church? Well, you have been very supportive of me. I suppose it's the least I could do. Sure, but next month and only if lunch is included."

"Deal. I'll be there on Friday morning for the verdict. Know that I'm praying for you and will stand with you no matter the outcome. Goodnight, Prudhoe," said Braedon.

His final words weighed heavily on Prudhoe, as she hung up the phone that night. As she searched her mind to understand why, she realized that there were two things pressing in on her. First, his words forced her to come to grips with the outcome, and she hadn't really thought that far ahead. What if her assailant was found not guilty? Worse—what if he wanted to retaliate against her for bringing charges? Fear began to set in. What if he wanted her dead? And if he was found guilty, would others from his clan want revenge? Maybe she'd be forced to leave town.

The only thing that tempered her fitful sleep that night was the second realization that she was beginning to think she might be able to trust Braedon. He certainly wasn't like other men she'd dated in the past. There was something much more settled and substantial to him, and it was comforting to her.

The next morning Prudhoe could barely respond to the alarm clock, but despite her physical and emotional exhaustion, she prepared for her court date. Not having much use for a closet full of clothes, owing to her usual uniformed existence, she wore the same brown suit and heels. The only pair of nylons she had had a small runner at the top, but she'd have to wear them and hope for the best.

Downing the last bit of coffee in her cup, she grabbed her keys and headed to her truck parked on her wide, treeless street. Another chilly fall day but nothing compared to what was to come, she thought. As she took in a deep breath before climbing into her truck, she could smell the freeze on its way.

This time the courthouse was warmer. Apparently, the workmen had accomplished their repairs. As she was slipping out of her truck carefully, so as not to put much more tension on that nylon stocking, she saw Braedon catching up to her.

"Good morning. You look tired. Are you doing alright?" he inquired.

"Not much sleep last night, but I'll be fine."

"Remember, no matter the outcome, you must not ever let this event define who you are or limit what you can do in the future, Prudhoe. Got it?"

"Yeah, well, it's already limited my walking around town, and I'm looking over my shoulder most of the time."

"You should be wise in matters of your safety, but the fears will subside over time. Now, walk with me, and hold your head up high."

As they entered the building, Shaw was just inside the door. Prudhoe introduced him to Braedon, and the two shook hands. The attorney then asked Braedon to go ahead and be seated in the courtroom as he'd escort Prudhoe from there.

Once again she felt nauseous just seeing the back of her assailant as they walked down the aisle of the courtroom. This time, he turned around and made eye contact. She glared back at him with a raging hatred in her heart. Her emotions were so powerful that she wished him dead. . . by her own hand. She was shaking by the time she was seated. As she looked down at her hands, her thoughts raced back and forth between smoldering anger and the small voice that reminded her that her hands were made for nursing. . . for caring. . . for healing.

Grateful for the distraction of the judge entering the courtroom and everyone standing, Prudhoe was able to get her emotions under control. Judge Hall went on about being the finder of fact as well as the determiner of guilt or innocence based on application of law and procedure. The lengthy preamble seemed interminable to Prudhoe. She just wanted to get this over with and run out of the courtroom, but she tried not to let her nerves show.

Finally, the judge asked the defendant to stand. Prudhoe knew his name, but had never spoken it, so hearing the judge state the name seemed to her way of thinking to be giving him too much respect. To Prudhoe, the rapist was akin to a dark, shadowy, vicious animal. Listening intently to every word, she heard the judge say, "On the basis of the facts and evidence provided at hearing, I have determined a verdict of guilty of forced rape in the first degree. The verdict carries with it a minimum eight-year to a twelve-year prison term. Because I believe you perjured yourself in my courtroom, I am sentencing you to the full twelve year maximum with parole review at ten years."

Chapter 19

Prudhoe was glad that she'd be spending another week in Juneau after the trial ended. She wanted nothing more than to be out of town and was looking forward to the change of scene. The quarterly trips were to keep her skills sharp in the medical transport arena. But her recent troubles had kept her from training this past summer. It was now early October, and she'd be heading to the capitol city to spend several days conursing a burn patient that would then need to be transferred to her hospital in Anchorage. Prudhoe was eager to learn as much as she could about people in such serious condition, who also faced many more struggles in the months and years ahead. However, she also knew that the care and transport would be very challenging from a nursing perspective.

She had chosen to arrive by float plane on Sunday because the weather looked better than it might be on Monday. And it was on that blustery, snowy morning that she was introduced to the nurses in the hospital run by a Catholic order of sisters. She threw herself into the work, which she found even more taxing than she had anticipated.

By Tuesday, however, she found herself thinking about Braedon. As she lay on her temporary-stay bed, staring out the window at the church steeple in front of the hospital, she wished she could talk to him about what she was learning and how things were going for him at the office. Her mind continually returned to his kindness and those dreamy brown eyes. She even made the decision that if he called in that "deal" to take her to church and lunch this month, she'd be ready.

When Friday morning came, Prudhoe mentally walked through the step-by-step and time-consuming work that would need to be done to transport the young patient from his bed in Juneau to his bed in Anchorage. It was backbreaking and difficult work, but the team pulled it off. And as Prudhoe sat with her sedated patient on the plane to Anchorage, she could feel the strain and stress in her body. It was also difficult not to think about the life-and-death situation on the flight last May. She was so grateful that Braedon was on that flight and, for a moment, wondered if his God had anything to do with that.

Sleeping in on Saturday, Prudhoe didn't wake until nearly eleven o'clock in the morning. As she spread out her newspaper and sipped her brew, the phone rang. She hoped it was Braedon, and she was right.

"Good morning, Nurse! How are you this fine Alaskan day?"

"Hey, you. I'm doing well, though it was an exhausting week. Oh, Braedon, I learned so much and got great marks on this transport. The staff at St. Ann's was very helpful and complimentary. I'm hoping my supervisor takes note. How are you doing?"

"I'm glad it went so well. And I bet the prayers of those nurses and nuns didn't hurt," said Braedon.

Prudhoe was silenced for a moment as she remembered walking in on a prayer circle of some of the nursing staff on her second day when she entered one of the laundry rooms. Though she didn't think much of it at the time, she was at once transported back to that small room and recalled the sense of peace she felt as they prayed for each of their patients by name.

"Uh, yeah, I suppose so. Say, that reminds me—are we going to your church service and lunch tomorrow?" Prudhoe inquired.

"Are you ready? I know I am ready to take you."

"Just tell me when I need to be ready tomorrow morning."

"Sure thing. I'll pick you up at nine forty-five. Meanwhile, I hope you have a restful day today. I've got a million things to do around this place before winter bites even harder. Glad you're home and safe, Prudhoe. See you tomorrow morning."

Prudhoe was spending her afternoon at Dika's place, as they had planned before her trip to Juneau. Packing up her beads, medallions, clasps, and other supplies to take with her, Prudhoe was looking forward to being with Dika, talking about everything and anything, and maybe even creating jewelry.

"This is so relaxing, Prudy. I think I would like to make some things for my family for Christmas," speculated Dika.

"Christmas is coming. I guess I should do something about seeing my mom. She really doesn't have anyone in this world but me and her sister. Perhaps I'll make them both something that I can give them. You know, I didn't even try to see her when I was over in Juneau last week. I'm such a bad daughter."

"Oh, Prudy, stop it. You're not a bad daughter as much as she is a bad mother. However, you should probably see her over the holiday. Can you afford to make the trip?"

"I always have money saved up to get over there. You know, in case there's a problem. But maybe I'll go for Thanksgiving this year."

"You still haven't told her, have you?"

"No, and I'm not sure that I will. It would break her heart, and she'd ask me to come live with her there. That's not something I'm about to do, but you're right, Dika, I should go see her."

Chapter 20

Prudhoe wasn't sure if she was appropriately dressed for church. It was now nine twenty-five, and she was still debating which skirt to wear. Finally deciding on the plain black pencil skirt with a white sweater, she started to work on her long hair. She thought perhaps she might wear it in a long braid down her back but wondered if she should instead attempt to look more Caucasian. Parting it in the center was typical for her, but today she found her only headband and pulled her hair back using that. It was a wide black headband made of plastic, but she had decorated it with colorful costume gems.

Ready by exactly nine forty-five, Prudhoe put on her gloves and black hooded coat with rabbit fur trim and headed out the door only to find Braedon walking up the sidewalk toward her. She was surprised to see he wasn't wearing a suit but instead had on a shirt, tie, and sweater. Now she was really confused about how fancy one was supposed to be for church.

"Hey, handsome. I hope I'm appropriately dressed for church this morning," said Prudhoe with tentativeness in her voice.

"You look lovely, as always. You don't need to worry about such things. I think you'll find people who attend the church come as they are. It's not about showing up for others but showing up for God."

As he helped her into the truck, which was made trickier by having to hike up her narrow skirt, Prudhoe caught him looking at her legs. He noticed that she noticed and quickly looked away.

"You're blushing again. What's the matter? Never seen a woman's legs before?"

"Of course I have. It's just that I suppose yours are of particular interest," he responded with his beautiful smile that revealed dimples to match his cleft chin.

As they drove to church, Prudhoe seemed to be returning to her old easy-going and jocular self. The two made small talk about where they would go for lunch and what Prudhoe could expect when she got to the church. Braedon briefed her on the pastor's name and the typical order of service so she would feel prepared.

When they arrived, Prudhoe was surprised to find the attenders were largely native peoples. Braedon was right; the people came as they were—some in older clothes, some in what were probably their best clothes. Most appeared to be of moderate means. It certainly wasn't a wealthy congregation, and the people greeted Braedon heartily as he walked in with Prudhoe and they took their seats in a middle row pew.

The service proceeded just as Braedon had indicated, though Prudhoe felt a step behind everyone with regard to standing up and sitting back down. She simply followed Braedon's cues and even snuggled into his side when he put his arm around her during the sermon.

The pastor spoke on something he called "the trinity." As he explained the triune nature of God—father, son, and spirit—Prudhoe was fascinated by the similarities she recalled from childhood when she heard her grandmother talk about such things. She remembered that Nuxalk religion included a belief in Alhkwntam, the father God, Manaakays, his son, and a spirit deity called Cmanwas. Throughout the remainder of the service, she wondered if there could possibly be a connection. She was determined to pursue further discussion of this three-in-one God with Braedon over lunch.

At the singing of the last hymn, which—like the others—Prudhoe had never heard, the people began milling around. It made Prudhoe a bit nervous, so she held Braedon's hand so that he could make any necessary introductions and explain their relationship to his friends. Heck, she thought, she didn't even know what their relationship really was, so it would be interesting to see how he defined it to others.

As they made their way to the door of the church, the pastor and his wife were shaking people's hands as each parishioner exited. Braedon looked over at Prudhoe while they piled up in what appeared to be a queue. His comforting glance seemed to suggest that this was normal and all was going to be fine. Upon nearing the door, Braedon stuck out his hand to shake the pastor's hand.

"Mr. Clarkson, good to see you again this morning. It appears you've brought a guest with you." the pastor observed.

"Yes, Pastor and Mrs. Williams, I'd like you to meet my friend Prudhoe Bonner. We met earlier this year. She's a nurse over at the hospital."

The older couple shook hands with Prudhoe and welcomed her warmly. They even encouraged her to return.

She thanked them, and before she knew it, the two were out the door and heading down the front stairs to return to Braedon's truck.

Not a word was said until Prudhoe had maneuvered herself back into the truck, using the running board to keep from having to hike her skirt too high. But once the two were settled into the truck and headed to the local diner for lunch, Prudhoe's nervousness vanished, and the conversation picked up.

"Well now, that wasn't so bad, was it?" Braedon asked.

"No, not bad. It was a bit different than what I was expecting. Oh, not that you didn't prepare me for the service, but there were other things...," Prudhoe said, with her thoughts left hanging.

"What other things?"

"I guess I didn't realize there would be so many native people—villagers—in attendance. Are they actually Christians?"

"Sure are. It's a great group of believers, Prudhoe. You see, in Christ we are all equal at the foot of the cross. His tribe consists of people from every nation, people all over the world who follow him and his word. The church isn't just one building; it's universal."

Prudhoe sat quietly and glanced over at Braedon's black leather Bible on the seat between them. For a second, she thought of that book as being the one thing that literally and figuratively came between them.

Arriving at the restaurant, they ducked in quickly because of the light rain that had started and found a booth in a quiet spot in the back. Over the meal, Prudhoe peppered Braedon with questions about the sermon, the church, and the Bible. It all seemed so foreign, and yet strangely familiar. Toward the end of their time together, Braedon told her that if she was seeking a relationship to the God of the universe, perhaps she could pray with him to accept Christ into her life.

"You mean me...pray like I see you doing over your food? Ah, I don't think I could do something like that in public, for all to see. In fact, I'm wondering if this whole religion thing is just too big of a dividing line for us. Perhaps we could just meet halfway and practice our own convictions in our own way. If we can't do that, perhaps we just aren't meant to continue seeing each other," Prudhoe concluded.

"Prudhoe, I'm afraid I can't practice my faith halfway. I'm sold out to Jesus Christ, and I've not concealed any of that from you. And your idea of not seeing each other unless I button up about it just reinforces my feelings that you're a serious flight risk. But if you are uncomfortable with who I am, I'll accept that."

Prudhoe didn't respond. Braedon paid the bill and then signaled readiness for departure in his usual confident manner. The ride in the truck that had been filled with chatter before lunch was now pretty quiet. And after Braedon helped her out of the truck and walked her to the door of her place, she gave him a friendly hug, took a step back, and said, "Braedon, thank you for lunch. I do think it might be best if we didn't try to force this subject any further. I have enjoyed our time together but leave it up to you to determine whether or not we should continue seeing each other."

CHAPTER 21

Prudhoe pulled her suitcase out of her truck to drop it off on the runway with the others. She felt the chill of thirty-nine degrees this morning as she boarded a small plane for Juneau to spend Thanksgiving with her mother. Her suitcase was small, but in her other hand, she had to carry a bag with a ten-pound, partially frozen turkey that she got from her employer. Thankful for the "bonus" that the hospital had given staffers for the holiday, she knew her mother would be grateful for it too. She'd been thawing it out in the refrigerator so that it would be ready to cook tomorrow and also offer leftovers for the few days they'd spend together.

Arriving a few hours later on the snow-dusted runway next to the channel, Prudhoe caught up with her mother who met her at the airfield.

"Prudy, my girl! I am so glad you came to be with me. My old car is nearby," said Bella.

Bella had just turned fifty, and Prudhoe couldn't help but notice her hair was even more ashen than when she last saw her. Her mother looked much older than her age, which Prudhoe chalked up to Bella's excessive drinking, as well as her decades of smoking before she gave it up a few years back. She also blamed the grueling work her mother did in the cannery. Bella had never finished grade school and was nearly illiterate, so despite it all, they were both grateful she had work.

Prudhoe put her suitcase and the turkey into the back seat, and they drove the few miles back to the town center where Bella rented a small apartment above a shop building on Main Street.

"I brought that turkey I told you about. It's small, but at least it was free," reminded Prudhoe.

"Goody. I have some potatoes we can roast, and I already made some bread and a pumpkin pie for us. So how have you been doing over in the big city with your important job?"

"Fine, Mom. I like Anchorage just fine. Your car sounds terrible. What's that knocking noise?"

"Oh yeah, I've been ignoring it because I don't have the money to fix it right now."

Prudhoe counted that comment as the first request for money and wondered how many more times she'd be confronted with Bella's "needs" over the next few days. The good news was that Bella didn't appear to have been drinking. Similarly, Prudhoe noticed that her mother seemed to steer clear of booze during their time together. However, Bella had inquired as to whether or not Prudhoe had met any marrying prospects in Anchorage.

"I have met one very nice man, but I'm afraid we haven't seen each other for about a month now. He's handsome, interesting, educated, successful, and kind. Unfortunately, we just aren't able to get past his religious convictions."

"What do you mean, Prudhoe? You know you can fall in love with a rich man just as easily as you can fall in love with a poor one. His religion doesn't really count for much. You can always go along to get along. That's what I always say."

"Well, it's just not quite that easy for me, Mom. And since he hasn't called in four weeks, I'm guessing it's not that easy for him either. He needs to find some nice white Christian girl, though I suspect they're hard to come by in Anchorage."

"You're counting the weeks?" her mother asked with one eyebrow raised.

By the time Sunday morning had arrived, Prudhoe was very ready to return home, taking her secret with her. However, the two had made some memories, and Prudhoe left her mother with fifty dollars in cash, which she characterized as a Christmas gift.

Bella's question about counting the weeks rolled around in Prudhoe's head all the way back to Anchorage on Sunday morning's flight. In fact, she had lots of questions. Glancing back and forth between the magazine on her lap and the small plane's portal window, she tried to convince herself that she didn't miss Braedon. Turning the page of the magazine, she looked at the Coca-Cola ad with multiple panels showing parents, happy children, and extended family bowing their heads in prayer over the Thanksgiving table. In that moment, she felt badly that on their last date she'd essentially accused Braedon of praying publicly in order to be seen. She realized that she was simply embarrassed when he did so...embarrassed of his God.

Chapter 22

Waking up at five o'clock in the morning with another nightmare was not how Prudhoe wanted to start her day off this Saturday. She thought the bad dreams were starting to diminish, but fear still gripped her when she recalled trying to scream with no success.

Deciding the best way to shake it off was to get up and start her routine, she made coffee and some toast and sat down to scratch out a list of things she needed to accomplish this weekend. Without giving it much thought, she added "find a Bible" to her list. When she looked down at the finished list, she was rather surprised by her curiosity about what might be in the Bible. She was particularly interested in the matter of prayer. The idea of talking to God seemed arrogant, but she wondered if that idea should be questioned... or perhaps tested.

By nine thirty, Prudhoe had read the paper, taken her shower, and dressed for the day when the phone rang. It was Dika, who wanted to see if she'd be around this morning so that she and Patuk could swing by to drop off some fish and meat for her freezer. It was not unusual for Patuk to go hunting and return with extra items for friends and family.

"I'm not about to turn that down. Yes, I'll be around this morning—just cleaning up and doing some laundry. Hey, Dika, I know this is going to sound like a weird question, but do you have a Bible?"

"Yes. I know Patuk has one that his grandmother gave him. It's around here somewhere. Why?"

"I'd like to look something up. Would you be willing to bring that with you when you stop by? I promise not to keep it for a long time. I can return it at work when we have lunch together later in the week," said Prudhoe.

"No problem. I'll bring it along. We'll see you around eleven or so."

When Dika and Patuk arrived at her door, Prudhoe gave them both a hug before walking out to their vehicle to help bring in the frozen haul. Loading up her freezer, they talked about her recent trip to see her mother.

"Went fine. Of course, I had to leave her some cash. But we had a nice Thanksgiving meal together. I'm glad I went," explained Prudhoe.

"I'm glad you went, Prudy. It means you'll be home for Christmas. You should come spend it with us! Hey, here's that Bible you asked for. Keep it as long as you like," said Dika.

After her friends departed, Prudhoe wandered back to her kitchen table where the Bible was left on the corner. It seemed to be drawing her, so she sat down and squared the Bible in front of her. Realizing she had no idea how to look something up or what was in the Bible, she decided to simply open the book to the approximate middle. The soft black leather-bound book opened to Psalm 116. Prudhoe read the words:

> I love the lord, because he hears my voice and
> my supplications.

> Because he has inclined his ear to me, therefore
> I shall call upon him as long as I live.

Prudhoe took the spoon on the table and placed it in the book at that spot and closed it. Sitting back in her chair, she was reeling from the words. It was as though they were just right, just in time, and just for her. So much so that before returning to read the entire Psalm, she did something she'd never done before—pray. Folding her hands in front of her and bowing her head, she uttered the words: "God, I don't know you, but I assume you know me. It feels strange to talk to you, but this book says you listen, so I'm calling upon you. If you are real, please show me truth. Amen."

As she lifted her head, Prudhoe looked around the room with anticipation of something, though she didn't know what. Her eyes fell on the telephone, and she considered calling Braedon to tell him what she'd done, but thought he might not care anymore.

Chapter 23

Prudhoe found herself spending most of the weekend returning to that Bible. She'd even found the inscription in front: "To my dear grandson Patuk. In here you'll find the wisdom of the ages. I am praying for you daily. With love from Grandma Sauri." Below this was a Bible verse from Psalm 119:9, which appeared to have been added later in a different ink: "Wherewithal shall a young man cleanse his way? By taking heed thereto according to thy word."

She made a mental note to ask Patuk about his grandmother. Then she remembered that Braedon had once told her that his favorite book in the Bible was 1 John, so she read the entire book. And though she found it difficult to understand, she was drawn to the verse in the first chapter that said, "If we confess our sins, he is faithful and just to forgive us our sins, and to cleanse us from all unrighteousness."

Monday and the workweek seemed to come so quickly. The days were long and made longer with the work involving the burn patient on their floor. Everything involved in caring for that patient seemed to take more time than she estimated, and most of the work required more than one nurse. Yet despite his extreme pain with burns covering nearly forty percent of his body, the patient was grateful and kind. In fact, on Wednesday of that week, Prudhoe made mention of his incredible endurance and tolerance. With tears streaming down his face, he told her that any strength he had was a coming from his Lord, Jesus Christ. It startled her. How could this young firefighter, who was perhaps all of twenty-five years old, be so sure...so humble?

Each night she returned to her apartment to eat dinner alone and pore over the scriptures. On Wednesday night, she stumbled across the scripture in the New Testament that said, "I can do all things through Christ who strengthens me." Though it was already dark outside, she got up from her chair and wandered outside into the nearly twenty degree weather without her coat. Fishing around in the barren yard outside her door, she found a flat, smooth stone, brought it inside, and wiped it clean with her sleeve. After inspecting it under the light, she went to her small dresser where she kept a felt-tip pen. Bringing the pen and the stone back to her kitchen table, she carefully wrote Philip 4:13 for she couldn't fit the whole name of Philippians on the stone. Besides, she figured the book might have been written by someone named Philip.

The next day Prudhoe placed the stone in the pocket of her uniform and proceeded to work. She waited until she knew there would be no other nurses in the burn patient's room. Slipping in, she found him asleep and figured it might be best if he didn't know anyway, as she quietly placed the marked stone on his nightstand by the phone.

That same night she returned home to eat some of the fish stew she'd made. With the Bible open beside her bowl, she continued to read well into the night. As she closed the book to go to bed, she paused for just a minute and looked up toward the ceiling. Quietly she prayed again—but just one question. "Is this truth?" Again, she looked around, wondering if there would be some kind of audible or visible response to her question. Nothing.

Friday had arrived, and Prudhoe was looking forward to the weekend. She had lunch with Dika in the cafeteria and asked her what she knew about Patuk's grandmother.

"Oh, I never knew her. Apparently, she died when he was about fifteen. I didn't meet Patuk until I was seventeen, and we were married as soon as I turned eighteen. He told me that she was a Christian and that she was his favorite grandparent because she was so very kind to him. She was Inuit like most of my relatives and his. Other than that, I don't know much about her. Why do you ask?"

"Well, I noticed her handwriting in the front of the Bible. My people believe that handwriting is a mark left forever, almost sacred. So it really caught my attention. Has Patuk ever read from that Bible?" Prudhoe inquired.

"I'm sure he has, but now that you mention it, I don't think it's been off the shelf for a few years. Why?"

"I just wondered, because his grandmother says it contains the wisdom of the ages. Does Patuk believe that?"

"I don't know, Prudy. You should ask him sometime... if I don't beat you to it," said Dika, with a wink as she shoved at Prudhoe's elbow.

As they got up to head back to their stations, Prudhoe informed Dika that she'd get the Bible back to her next week because she'd decided to get her own.

That afternoon, she and another coworker spent hours working on the burn patient's wounds again. His pain was clearly evident on his face, yet he never cried out, not even a whimper. When Prudhoe returned after the process to give him his pain medications, he swallowed them and caught her glancing at his nightstand.

"You put that stone there, didn't you?"

Startled by his question but knowing she must be honest with him, she spoke a quiet "yes."

"Thank you. I will keep it long after I've left the hospital. I figured you must know truth."

Chapter 24

On Saturday, Prudhoe was cooking, cleaning, and laundering her uniforms for the following week. It was a pretty typical routine for her, but nothing about this day seemed typical. She just kept thinking about what her patient had said the day before. He hadn't seen the tears she shed in the bathroom after leaving his room. After all, she'd prayed that God would show her the truth, and the patient had confirmed where it could be found. Furthermore, she knew that if Christ could strengthen this man in his suffering, he could surely strengthen her after what she'd been through.

When Sunday arrived, Prudhoe put on her warmest outfit and set out in her truck for the Methodist church. She purposely planned to be a few minutes late so she could enter without any fanfare or introductions. The front doors were already closed as she walked up the few stairs to open one of the doors and slip in. Seeing Braedon sitting alone on the outside of the fifth pew on the right, she waited until everyone stood to sing a hymn. Making her way to the pew, she gently pushed him to the inside and began trying to sing the words in the hymnal he was holding. She secretly wished she'd had a picture of his surprised face at that moment, but he continued singing. After the "amen" at the end of the song, he helped her with taking her coat off, and they sat close to each other during the service.

After the sermon, which was taken from one of the many Bible books that contained the name John that Prudhoe had read, things were starting to make a bit more sense to Prudhoe. She hadn't remembered getting as far as John 17, so it almost took her breath away when one of the parishioners read the words, "Sanctify them through thy word; thy word is truth." It was all the confirmation she needed to know that God had answered her meager prayer request made just a week earlier. So when the pastor asked for anyone who wanted to come forward to make their confession of belief or request baptism, Prudhoe stepped out of the pew and made her way quickly to the front. She was initially surprised to find she was the only one who went forward, but she was not embarrassed. In fact, it was more like a strange mix of feeling triumphant and humbled at the same time.

Pastor Williams welcomed Prudhoe and prayed for her in the front of the church, and then he reminded the congregation of the significance of such a public profession of faith by quoting a Bible verse from the book of Mark that Prudhoe wasn't even aware of: "Whosoever therefore shall confess me before men, him will I confess also before my Father which is in heaven."

By the time the service was over, Prudhoe found herself surrounded by many congregants who were shaking her hand or giving her a hug. These people who seemed so strange to her were now like newfound family. And there they were—Inuit, Tlingit, Haida, Caucasian, Yupik, and now Nuxalk—all united under one banner who was Christ.

Hanging back in the crowd was Braedon, who looked even more handsome than she remembered. It had been over six weeks since she'd seen him, and he looked so good to her. He made his way toward her and showing no inhibition, he put his arms around her so tightly that her face smashed against his thick parka. However, the smell of that familiar aftershave was once again a comfort to her. When he stepped back to look at her, it appeared that there were tears barely holding onto the bottom lids of his eyes.

"Prudhoe, I'm happy for you. May I take you to lunch, and you can tell me what brought you to this decision. I mean, I know who brought you to it, but I want to hear all about these last months."

"Months? Hey now, it's only been six weeks, big guy."

"I guess it seems like a lot longer to me. I've missed your spunky ways. I've thought of you many times but felt restrained from calling you," Braedon confessed.

"I guess it was just not the right timing before. But who knows, maybe the second time around might be better," said Prudhoe with clear hope in her voice.

Before the two left the musty, old church, Pastor Williams brought forth a Bible still wrapped in plastic. He handed it to Prudhoe, but she almost didn't take it saying, "I was going to buy one for myself. I'm a working girl. Maybe you should give this one to someone who can't afford one."

"Prudhoe, take it. It's a gift from the church. It's the most important operator's manual you'll need for this Christian life," said the pastor with a broad smile.

Heading out to their respective vehicles, Prudhoe and Braedon agreed to meet at the same diner they went to when they last saw each other. As Prudhoe drove out of the parking lot, she felt she'd never been so happy in all her days on this earth.

CHAPTER 25

As Braedon rolled down the passenger side window of his truck parked in the diner parking lot, Prudhoe got her first look at his loyal canine, Bozo, who never took his eyes off Braedon.

"He seems a bit concerned about having me around," said Prudhoe, as she carefully petted Bozo's head.

"He is kind of a one-person dog, but he's friendly. It will take a few visits for him to get used to you. Shall we dine?"

"Sure, I didn't have breakfast this morning, so I'm definitely hungry!"

As the couple strolled through the door, the waitress grabbed menus and showed them to the same quiet booth they'd been in weeks earlier. They ordered their lunch, and immediately Braedon inquired about what Prudhoe had been up to for all those weeks.

"So much has happened, Braedon. First, I went to see my mother in Juneau over Thanksgiving. We got along pretty well and made a fine meal together. Oh, and that was my second trip to Juneau recently because I was also there in October for some more training. I went to spend the week learning about how to care for burn patients so that I could also handle the airlift of a patient over to our own hospital here. We've been taking care of him since. He's getting better each week, but the pain levels are severe."

"My, that's awful. He's fortunate to have you as his caregiver though. I'm also glad you had a good time with your mother. Now tell me more about these weeks. I can't get enough of you...I mean, I want to hear more," said Braedon.

"What you probably want to know is how I came to my decision this morning. You're probably also wondering if it's authentic. I assure you that it is. It's like you said—prayer is just talking to God. And he answered me!"

"He always answers prayer, Prudhoe; just not always the way we think he should. But tell me about your prayer," prodded Braedon.

"Well, I borrowed a friend's Bible and decided to look up something about prayer, but I had no idea where to start or what was in there. I opened it up to what I thought was the middle and started to read in Psalms. It said something about how he hears us, so I thought I'd test him on that by asking him to show me truth. Nothing happened right away, but I spent the rest of the weekend reading things in the Bible. Then when I went back to work last week, one day I told that burn patient how brave he was. He told me that any strength he had came from Jesus Christ."

"Wow, that's amazing faith you were witnessing, Prudhoe. By the way, I noticed that your friend Dika calls you Prudy. Is that privilege reserved only to her, or do you consider me enough of a friend that I can call you that?" asked Braedon, as their food arrived at the table.

"Of course you are that kind of friend. Now are you going to pray over this meal for us, or do I have to?"

Braedon smiled and winked at her before he bowed his head and prayed.

"Father God, I praise you for drawing my friend to your side by the power of the Holy Spirit. I now pray that you will sanctify her by your word. And let me be a help to her in whatever way I can. Thank you for this food, and please bless it to our bodies. In the name of Jesus, I pray. Amen."

Prudhoe went on to tell Braedon about the stone that she marked with the verse from Philippians, and how the patient figured out it was her who put it on his nightstand. She told him that the man said he knew she must "know truth."

"So God confirmed for me, through the verses, prayer, and the Christian man's statement, that Jesus had shown me truth. It was what I asked of him, and he did it," said Prudhoe with increasing excitement in her voice.

Once again, Braedon smiled broadly with his fork full of food. As he lowered the fork back to his plate, he said, "Prudy, in this, he answered my prayers too."

CHAPTER 26

Amidst the clanging of trays and utensils, Dika sat down next to Prudhoe at their usual spot in the cafeteria on Monday afternoon.

"Did you swallow a bird or something? You look positively wild-eyed today. What's up?" asked Dika.

"Who, me? Well, I just wanted you to hear about my good news. In fact, I have lots of good news," announced Prudhoe.

"Go! I'll eat while you talk. I'm so hungry," said Dika, as she dove into her meal.

"Well, first of all, I brought the Bible back. I don't need it anymore because I have one of my own now. I got it yesterday when I went to the Methodist church."

"Are you chasing Braedon because you still think he's playing hard-to-get?"

"No. I went because I prayed that God would show me the truth. I read the Bible you lent me. It made sense to me. Then at church yesterday, I gave my life to Christ," responded Prudhoe in a very matter-of-fact tone.

"You did what? Prudy, Braedon's not worth getting religion for. That's rather extreme, don't you think?"

"Dika, it's not about him. It's about me. I became a Christian," repeated Prudhoe, while putting emphasis on each of those last words.

"Okay, Prudy. I'm glad to hear that...I guess. What else is in the good news package?"

"That's the best news, but I also didn't tell Braedon about my decision. I just showed up at the church and listened to the sermon. Then when the pastor asked if anyone wanted to come forward for confession and eventual baptism, I practically ran down to the front. I think Braedon was pretty surprised, but very happy for me. Then we went to lunch, and I told him all about God's answers to my prayer. He told me he'd been praying for me. He even told me that he'd prayed that God would send someone into my life that would help me understand. And that prayer was answered too, in the form of one of my patients."

"That's interesting. What else?" Dika insisted.

"Well, at the end of our time together, he walked me to my car and asked me to consider the matter of courting."

"What's that mean?"

"He said it means he wants us to date each other exclusively with the intent to find out if we might want to take the relationship further," explained Prudhoe.

"You mean have sex?"

"No, Dika. I told you he's an honorable guy. He's nothing like the men I've dated in the past. And I don't want men like that now anyway. Dika, I think Braedon is a very caring man, who just happens to be extremely good-looking too!"

"So let me get this straight. Is this courting thing supposed to be like pre-engagement or something? Or would you two already be engaged if you're courting?"

"I don't know all the ins and outs of it. I just know that I told him I would pray about it, and he said he would. He's going to call me later this week to see where I stand."

"Well, Prudy, it all sounds kinda strange but also kinda sweet. I just want you to be happy, and you seem to be happier than I've seen you in some time," noted Dika.

As the days passed, Braedon was true to his word. On Thursday evening, he called.

"Evening, Prudy. Is this a good time to talk?"

"Sure is. I could hardly wait for you to call, and I resisted calling you to tell you that I'm ready to start courting."

There was husky laughter on the other end of the phone.

"Are you laughing at me?" Prudhoe asked.

"Never at you. It's just that you make me laugh with your straightforward ways. You're definitely one who doesn't hide her feelings or thoughts. It's one of the things I find endearing about you, Prudy. And, by the way, I'm ready to start courting too. How about tomorrow night we take in a movie after work?"

Chapter 27

With Christmas approaching, Braedon asked Prudhoe to travel to Thane to spend the holiday week with his parents. Though Prudhoe had to work day shift on Christmas Day, she was able to take a few days off earlier in the week. Braedon made plans for her to travel by plane with him to Juneau on Monday, and then he would put her back on a plane on Thursday—Christmas Eve—while staying behind to spend Christmas with his parents. They had also decided to spend time in Juneau with her mother before his parents picked them up to drive the few miles down the road to Thane. Similarly, Braedon would return Prudhoe to Juneau a few hours earlier than her flight on Christmas Eve so that she could visit with her mother again before returning to Anchorage.

Prudhoe was getting excited about her vacation plans. She looked forward to introducing her mother to Braedon, to meeting his parents, and to having a Christmas dinner with Dika and Patuk after working that day. She was also looking forward to discharging her burn patient to the care of his local family members, who had taken turns visiting him almost every day in the hospital. He still had a long road of recovery ahead of him, but his steady optimism and gratitude for life had been an inspiration to the whole staff. Of course, none had been more impacted by his presence than Prudhoe, who had recently taken the time to explain to him what that impact meant in her life.

Prudhoe and Braedon boarded the small plane to Juneau on the evening of Monday, December 21 and were chatty all the way along the short flight.

"Are you nervous to meet my parents?" he asked.

"Not really, though I do wonder if you've told them I'm native," responded Prudhoe with no small measure of curiosity.

"Yes, they know that now. They are strong Christians, and they know that Old Testament scripture tells us that God made all the nations from a single drop of blood. You don't have to worry about them. Should I be concerned about meeting your mom?"

"No, she's pretty excited about meeting you actually. Her issues are with men in general because she's had such bad experiences. First, it was my father who left us and later drank himself to death. Then, it was a series of men she lived with, each of whom treated her poorly. She's now fifty years old and has given up on men altogether in these last seven or eight years, but I think she drinks out of loneliness."

"How do you think she'll feel about your decision for Christ?" Braedon asked.

"I think she'll give us a wide berth on that but probably won't tolerate attempts to talk to her about it. You have to remember that lots of native people connect their heritage with their spiritualism. In other words, they often don't separate those two things."

"Now I'm even more nervous about meeting her. I hope she doesn't think that you've betrayed your heritage by becoming a Christian. However, I'm very happy about this time we have together," said Braedon as he reached over to hold her hand.

"Braedon, I appreciate that you laid down a "no gifts" rule with your parents for this trip. I know everyone would feel awkward about exchanging Christmas presents with people they don't yet know very well. And heaven knows, I sure don't want to step in it on anything else. So can you tell me what other things you've told your parents about me?"

"I told them how we met and gave them a brief summary of your heritage and upbringing. Also, I told them that you are a nurse, that you are a new convert to Christianity, that you're attending my church, and that we're in a courtship process. In other words, they know we are serious. Does any of that concern you?" he asked.

"No, none of that," stated Prudhoe hesitatingly.

As sensitive as Braedon was to her already, he immediately knew what she meant by her line of questioning.

"Prudy, it's not up to me to tell them what happened this spring, about the court case, or anything else of a deeply personal nature. I leave that up to you to share as you feel ready—with my parents, with your mother, and even with me. But remember this one thing: you bear no shame for the sin that was committed against you. It may take time for you to accept that, but I can assure you that God sees you as blameless in Christ…and so do I."

Prudhoe visibly dropped her shoulders in relief. She wasn't ready to talk about any of those hideous things with anyone during the course of this trip.

By the time they had touched down in Juneau, it was a few degrees warmer than Anchorage, but snow was beginning to fall. The couple quickly picked up their small overnight bags and headed over to the parking area, where Prudhoe spotted her mother immediately.

"Mom, I want you to meet Braedon Clarkson. Braedon, meet my mother, Bella Bonner."

"Good to finally meet you Mrs. Bonner," said Braedon, as he stuck out his hand to shake hers.

"Sure, sure. Very glad to meet you too. You can call me Bella. No need to be so proper around me. Well, you're just as handsome as Prudy said you are."

Prudhoe scowled at her mother as they all proceeded to get into the warm idling Plymouth. It was Bella's excessive drinking, fast talking, and loose lips that embarrassed her daughter the most when she was growing up, but she loved her mother despite it all.

It was nearly eight o'clock at night, and no one had eaten.

"Miss Bonner…I mean, Bella," Braedon started after clearing his throat. "Is there any place open where I could buy you ladies a late dinner before my folks arrive to pick us up at nine?"

As Bella drove over the old depression-era bridge into the heart of town, she indicated there was a small place near the docks that was open late. That was a perfect spot since Mr. and Mrs. Clarkson had agreed to pick them up on Front Street.

Though Braedon was clearly nervous about meeting Prudhoe's mother, it was probably worse for Bella. Prudhoe could tell that her mother had taken the edge off her own nerves by drinking. The smell of beer was something she couldn't miss, though she hoped that Braedon didn't notice. Despite that, the two seemed to hit it off just fine, and by the time they'd finished their modest meals, the snow had let up.

Driving just a few blocks to the Capitol Theater, Braedon could see the family vehicle on the street with his folks staying warm inside. The narrow streets meant Bella would have to double park just long enough for the couple to get their things and transfer over to the next car. There was not much time for long goodbyes, but they managed. Prudhoe hugged her mother and reminded her she'd see her on the return trip.

As the two settled into the back seat of the Clarkson car, Braedon was already making introductions all around while simultaneously waving goodbye out the window at Mrs. Bonner.

CHAPTER 28

Bringing up the rear, Braedon carried their bags as he and Prudhoe entered the warm wood-paneled home where he'd grown up. Jack and Joanne Clarkson followed the couple into the house from the large outbuilding that doubled as Jack's workshop, where they had parked the car.

Prudhoe immediately felt their cozy hospitality as they took her coat and carried her things to the guest bedroom. Braedon placed his duffle in the room where he grew up, the room Joanne hadn't changed for over ten years. It still contained his old ribbons, trophies, and sports paraphernalia from childhood days. The guest room, on the other hand, was clean and sparsely decorated and appeared to double as Joanne's sewing room.

As the four regrouped back in the living room, Joanne invited everyone to sit at the dining room table just off the kitchen. She acknowledged that it was getting late, but she'd made Braedon's favorite dessert, a berry slump.

"Oh, Prudy, you're gonna love this," said Braedon, while rubbing his hands together.

"I'm sure I will," she acknowledged, as he held the chair for her to sit down at the table.

"I hope you do, Prudhoe. This reminds me, we've heard Braedon refer to you as Prudhoe and as Prudy. Which do you prefer dear?" Joanne inquired.

"Prudy is something my friends and family call me. And I feel I'm among those here, so please feel free to call me Prudy."

The foursome had a lovely evening talking about Prudhoe's job as well as what Braedon was up to at the land office. At around ten thirty, they all retired for the night with plans for an early rising to do some late-season hunting.

Prudhoe dragged herself out of bed at six o'clock in the morning to be at the breakfast table on time. Mrs. Clarkson was going to be staying behind to prepare food for a big dinner that night because Prudhoe had so few days with them. She was also preparing the freezers to receive any meat that might be brought home that evening.

After a hearty breakfast, Prudhoe, Braedon, and Mr. Clarkson headed out with their gear, hoping for a deer. However, it wasn't until around noon that Braedon found tracks and scat from an elk. The team had intentionally passed a large bull earlier, knowing that they couldn't haul out the over four hundred pounds of meat that it represented. However, these tracks appeared to be smaller so they followed them through to an open meadow where they spotted an elk cow. Mr. Clarkson made a single clean shot in the neck that dropped the elk in place. Now the work began because they'd have to watch for bear while gutting the elk, which would still yield close to two hundred pounds of large meat pieces on the bone. They'd leave behind parts that bears might want as they prepared for the long winter. It was a long afternoon with Prudhoe standing watch while the men dressed out the kill.

Upon arriving back home around six thirty in the evening, Mrs. Clarkson was surprised to see how much meat needed to be butchered. At the dinner table, they decided to share some with the neighbor. It was a wonderful meal of venison, roasted potatoes, cornbread stuffing, pickled vegetables, and a platter full of Christmas cookies for dessert. Over coffee and cookies, Mr. Clarkson read the Christmas story from scripture. Prudhoe loved it. Even though she remembered bits and pieces from hearing the story in the past, she'd never really concentrated on the details before.

After dinner, the men went to the outbuilding to perform the tedious work of butchering the meat and packing the freezers. While they were busy, Prudhoe and Mrs. Clarkson had time to clean up the table and kitchen while chatting. Prudhoe heard stories about Braedon's youthful antics and how he had come to accept Jesus as his savior in his teens. Joanne Clarkson proudly showed off a bookcase full of Braedon's wrestling and marksmanship trophies, along with certificates of academic merit from high school. Prudhoe found all of it fascinating, while also feeling a bit envious about how secure Braedon's childhood had been. Whenever Joanne asked Prudhoe about her childhood, she was very sensitive in her questions and responses and always pointed Prudhoe to her new life in Christ. It was a time of bonding for the two women. And when Joanne took a moment to pray for her, Prudhoe's tears flowed throughout.

"Lord, I thank you for my new sister in Christ, Prudhoe Bonner. I ask that you place a hedge of protection around her newfound faith so that it will flourish in her heart and mind. Give her a hunger for your Word and a desire to serve you always. Remind her that she is a new creation in you and that all along you have been fitting her for heaven.

Thank you for all the believers you have sent into her life to testify to your saving grace. Thank you that you gave her eyes to see and ears to hear and that, no matter what happens, you will bear her up on eagle's wings as you've promised. In Jesus's name. Amen."

On their last full day together in Thane, there was quite a bit of snowfall, and the temperature had dropped. The four played cards and board games while snacking on the leftovers from the night before. That evening Mr. Clarkson held Bible study by the fireplace, and Prudhoe hung on every word as he covered the small book of Jude. She sat close to Braedon on the couch as his father read the scripture, and she loved to hear that she would one day "stand blameless" in the presence of a holy God because of Christ, who paid her way to freedom.

On Christmas Eve day, it was just after breakfast when Braedon carried her bag to the car to drive her back to Juneau. Prudhoe could tell that he wasn't too thrilled to see her go after these concentrated days of getting to know each other better. After saying her thank-yous and goodbyes to his parents, who hugged her tightly before sending her off, the couple drove in silence for the first mile towards town. It was Braedon who broke the silence first.

"I wish you could stay through the weekend, but I understand that duty calls. I'll miss having you here, Prudy."

"What will you miss?" asked Prudhoe, who was fishing hard to learn how he felt about their relationship at this point.

"I'll miss your beautiful but curious smile, almost Mona Lisa-like. I'll miss your confident and capable personality. I'll miss holding your hand under the dining table too," Braedon said without taking his eyes off the road.

Staring at the handsome driver, she whispered, "I like being with you too."

Prudhoe and her mother spent a few hours together before she had to get back on a plane. During that time, they shared a meal and exchanged gifts. Prudhoe insisted on doing the driving to the airstrip because she was concerned that Bella had already had too much to drink, even before she'd been dropped off by Braedon. However, Bella seemed genuinely appreciative of the beautiful necklace that her daughter had made for her and was also happy to get some cash. Prudhoe hadn't expected anything in return, because of her mother's modest means, but a few cans of fish ended up in her purse anyway.

CHAPTER 29

Christmas Day on the intensive care unit in the hospital was pretty quiet, though plenty of family members were coming and going throughout Prudhoe's shift. She ate very little at lunchtime so that she would be plenty hungry for dinner at Dika's that evening. She had so much to tell them and could hardly wait to spend time with her and Patuk.

Arriving around six o'clock, Prudhoe was holding two gift-wrapped items and a jar of pickles when Dika opened the door.

"Merry Christmas, Dika!" said Prudhoe, as she came out of the cold and breezed into the hallway.

"Prudy, you didn't have to bring anything with you. We're the ones who invited you for dinner."

"You know me, Dika; I don't like to arrive empty-handed to a party! The place smells yummy. When do we eat?"

"Won't be long now. You can drop things on the dining table, and come into the kitchen with me and Patuk so we can hear about your trip to Juneau."

After dropping the gifts and pickles off at the table, Prudhoe proceeded to the kitchen and hugged Patuk before he returned to mashing some potatoes in a pot. Both Patuk and

Dika peppered Prudhoe with questions about her mother, Braedon, his parents, his home, and more. The conversation was nonstop, even as the three carried food to the table and sat down. Then Prudhoe stopped everyone from starting to dig in by asking if she could pray over the food. Dika looked over at Patuk and shrugged her shoulders, resulting in Patuk telling her to go ahead and pray.

"Lord, I am still not very good at this praying thing, but thank you for this wonderful food and these wonderful people. Please look upon us with your favor now and into next year. Amen."

By the end of the meal, Dika finally asked the question that she really wanted an answer to.

"Prudy, are you in love with Braedon? Is he in love with you?"

"Dee, I can't answer that last question, but I can assure you that I'm being careful on the first one. I don't want to get burned, yet he seems so sincere and caring. He's just not like any other man I've met."

"I think you need to test him. I did that with Patuk, you know!"

"You did? What did you do to him?" Prudhoe asked.

Patuk interrupted with his chuckling. "She told me she wanted to date other men, just when I had decided I was ready to make my serious move."

"Oh, Dika, you didn't. What happened?"

"He called my bluff and told me I could do that, but then I'd miss out on a lifetime with him!" responded Dika with a big smile on her face.

"Well, maybe I'll try testing him, but I don't think I can try your approach while we're courting," claimed Prudhoe.

Prudhoe thoroughly enjoyed the meal, the board game afterwards, and Dika's face when she saw the matching bracelet, earrings, and necklace handmade just for her. Patuk also seemed to appreciate the beaded belt Prudhoe made for him. The threesome had a great evening together, yet all three were looking forward to sleeping in the next morning.

In fact, Prudhoe spent Saturday doing her household chores, and then she attended church on her own the next day. She still felt a bit awkward sitting in the church by herself, but the sermon was reassuring of her newfound faith. The pastor opened up new scriptures for her. During the time of silence, Prudhoe prayed for Braedon's safe return that afternoon, for Dika and Patuk, and for herself.

By Monday morning, Prudhoe was refreshed and ready for her shift work, much of which was routine. Around lunchtime, she saw Braedon coming down the hallway. Her heart jumped for joy in seeing that familiar stride.

"Hey, I thought I'd have lunch with you in the cafeteria. I'll head down there and wait for you if you have things you need to finish," he said, as he approached her and gave her quick hug when no one was watching.

"So glad you thought of that. I'll meet you down there in five minutes," said Prudhoe through her radiant smile.

Once the two got through the cafeteria line with their slotted food trays and found a quiet table for two in the corner, Braedon held her hand and said a quick prayer.

"You look even prettier than I remember," he said.

"I missed you too. I hope the rest of your holiday was good. Parents okay?"

"They sure are. They really like you, Prudy...but not as much as I do," Braedon said, winking at her. "Oh, I don't want to forget. I know we weren't supposed to do Christmas gifts, so we'll just call these supplies."

Pulling a paper bag from his parka and placing it in on the table, he nodded at her to open it. Prudhoe opened the top of the bag and peeked in. Immediately overtaken by a wonderful hickory smell, she pulled out the clear bag inside the paper bag.

"Wow, you made jerky? Now that's romantic," Prudhoe teased.

"Okay, maybe not so romantic, but I worked hard on those elk strips, thinking they might remind you of our hunting trip together last week."

"It's a wonderful thought, Braedon. I love jerky and knowing you made it will make it taste even better," she assured him.

"It's not exactly like we live in a place where I can easily obtain fresh-cut roses for you, so this will have to do."

"It'll more than do. Thank you very much."

As they were eating, Braedon also mentioned that there was a Bible study at the church on Wednesday nights, except during the month of December.

"They'll be starting up again on January 6. It's a week from Wednesday. I believe one of the elders will be teaching from the book of Matthew as well as some Old Testament passages. Do you think you might like to go with me?" he inquired.

"Sure thing, it's a date. Oh wait, it's a courtship!"

CHAPTER 30

The first Wednesday night Bible study started at six thirty at the church. Braedon's truck was in front of Prudhoe's place exactly fifteen minutes before they needed to be at the church. She made sure to bring her new Bible with her. As they drove to the church, the two talked about how things were going at work before the subject turned to the study.

"How many people usually attend this Bible study?" inquired Prudhoe.

"It varies by quarter; we had about a dozen last quarter. It seems to grow by one person each quarter. Perhaps you'll be our one newcomer this time."

"I brought a small notebook and a pen to take notes, but..." Her voice trailed off as she reached over to flip through the pages of his Bible sitting on the seat. "Hey, it looks like you have written things in your Bible. Is that allowed?"

"Of course. Your new Bible is going to become like your home each time you enter it. You'll want memories in that home, especially those things that God has brought to your attention as you learn about him. Think of those things as pictures you hang on the walls of your home. Fresh insight, life application, or even thanksgiving or praise to him—they can all go in there. Give yourself permission to start tonight."

"Okay. I just thought maybe it was something sacred, so you couldn't write on it," explained Prudhoe.

"His word is sacred all right, but maybe not the margins!"

When they pulled up to park, he shut off the truck and turned to face her. In that moment, Prudhoe could feel heat rising upon her cheeks, even in the middle of winter. There was no doubt she was attracted to Braedon's winsome and wise soul, but she also felt the attraction of his being so close to her. He must have been feeling the same way because he leaned toward her and touched her lips with his index finger and then proceeded to kiss them gently. This kiss was like fireworks going off, despite the frigid, black, and starry night outside. She could sense that she was falling for him, but it was tempered by her fears of hurt and betrayal. She must keep herself in reserve, she thought, because no man could be fully trusted.

The Bible study started with introductions, coffee, tea, and store-bought cookies. Within fifteen minutes, the pastor had called the group together for prayer, after welcoming Prudhoe to the group. Pastor Williams reminded everyone that Bible study should always start with prayer to ask the Spirit of God to reveal his truth to the reader. The study itself was informative. Prudhoe took some notes on her notepad and also dared to write a few things in the margins of her new Bible. Sitting very close to Braedon meant she could feel the vibration of his voice in his chest whenever he spoke or asked a question. Somehow that felt reassuring to her.

The pastor asked the attendees to consider the previous week's question about why they should forgive those who have wronged them. Most of the class conceded that it was difficult sometimes. Still they knew that the Lord had forgiven them, and they were to be imitators of him. Williams reread out loud the verse from Ephesians from the earlier lesson:

"And be kind to one another, tender-hearted, forgiving each other, just as God in Christ also has forgiven you."

"Now tonight I want to focus on how we can do that. What gives us the ability to forgive? Some of you here may have been so deeply wronged that you see forgiving akin to flying," the kind pastor acknowledged. He then went on to talk about how it is the Spirit of God dwelling in a believer that gives them the ability to fly—to forgive. Pastor Williams referred to this dwelling as "gospel wings." The term came from a poem he read to the group. It was written by John Bunyan, a nonconformist preacher, who spent many years in jail in England for his faith.

Run, John, run, the law commands
But gives us neither feet nor hands,
Far better news the gospel brings:
It bids us fly and gives us wings.

Prudhoe sat fascinated by the brief and difficult history of Bunyan that the pastor recounted. But it was a quote from another preacher that really had Prudhoe stirred up inside. She could feel resistance rising in her as Pastor Williams quoted a man named Charles Spurgeon.

"To be forgiven is such sweetness that honey is tasteless in comparison with it. But yet there is one thing sweeter still, and that is to forgive. As it is more blessed to give than to receive, so to forgive rises a state higher in experience than to be forgiven."

After a brief closing prayer at the end of class, the group broke up, and Prudhoe and Braedon headed back to the truck. There were a few minutes of silence before Prudhoe piped up with a question.

"Braedon, the pastor said that Christians are to forgive much because we have been forgiven much. I think I understand that, but isn't there a limit to that? Do I have to forgive. . . ," she began, but her voice trailed off. She turned to look out the passenger side window.

"Yes, Prudy, even him. You aren't required to accept the evil perpetrated upon you. God doesn't accept it, though he may use it by calling you to help others. You'll need to be ready for that, so you can't carry the hatred forward into your new life with Christ. It will only be a burden and a stumbling block to your spiritual growth," counseled Braedon.

"Does that mean you have forgiven him?" asked Prudhoe.

"His sin was against God and against you. I admit I was enraged with him and wanted God to vindicate you by punishing him. But I realized that I had to let the anger go, and I believe God has and is punishing him. But I also admit that I've only prayed for him once. . . over this last holiday."

"Well, it's not punishment enough as far as I'm concerned. And I sure as hell can't pray for him," Prudhoe stated, as she folded her arms across her chest in defiance.

Things were quiet for many seconds before Braedon said, "You can be sure that hell doesn't want you to pray for him."

By the time they arrived back at Prudhoe's place, there was a stony silence in the truck.

Braedon walked Prudhoe to her front door and reached out to put his arms around her. She resisted his bear hug and said under her breath, "I can't trust any of you men. You're all the same."

Braedon swallowed hard as he took a step back. Staring at her for what seemed like forever, he finally spoke. "Prudy, I want to win your trust because I love you. No matter how much you push me away, the shelf life of my love for you will be eternal."

With that, he turned to walk back to his truck and drive off into the dark night as Prudy closed and locked her front door.

Chapter 31

Friday was a long day at the hospital for Prudhoe. Not only did they have a full house, but they also were short staffed because the charge nurse was in meetings most of the day. Prudhoe was even called in to work an extra shift on Sunday. While her mind and body were occupied with work, she couldn't help but wonder if Braedon would be showing up on her doorstep again this Wednesday evening for Bible study. The discussion on forgiveness, as well as their parting, was eating away at her. She caught herself thinking about how different things would have been just a month or so ago. None of this would have bothered her. She would have just shaken it off, perceiving herself to be strong. Now she felt weak when thinking of the strength of Braedon's faith and commitment.

Though she didn't hear from him over the weekend, Wednesday did arrive, and so did Braedon. Just as he was about to knock on her front door, Prudhoe opened it, greeted him, and tucked her Bible under her arm so she could lock the door. As they walked to the truck, he offered his arm because of the icy sidewalk. Carefully, they made their way in the chilly wind of the night.

"I wasn't sure you'd want to be with me this evening," said Prudhoe.

"Of course I do. I hope we can spend lots of evenings together. I'm not going to be that easy to kick to the curb."

As they got into the idling truck, it wasn't just the heater running that seemed to warm things up. Prudhoe leaned over to kiss Braedon on the cheek before he put his truck in drive.

"What's that for?"

"I'm sorry about last week. My attitude was pretty bad. I have prayed about it because nothing about it felt right. I can't blame you for the bad things that have happened to me in my life. You were right about moving forward in my new life. In fact, until you said that last week, I hadn't even thought about God doing a new thing in my life. I read more from the Bible, and now I understand that it's not just about getting into heaven. I belong to Jesus now. He's not just for later."

"Yep, and he belongs to you. That's a pretty significant breakthrough—something only the Spirit of God could reveal to you. I'm glad for your understanding because I'm a sinner too. I'm going to mess up because we're all imperfect. So even my profession of love is going to be less than perfect. That's why you'll need to keep your eyes on Christ, who never leaves nor forsakes."

"Oh yeah, about that profession of love. I assume you mean in the way the pastor was talking about it last week—that you love me like a sister in Christ, right?"

"I do love you that way too," said Braedon.

Prudhoe quickly looked over at him as he stared straight ahead.

"Why, Braedon Clarkson, I do believe you're blushing again."

As they drove to the church, they talked about their challenges at work and home. They both also confessed that they missed each other and wanted to always quickly mend rifts in their relationship going forward.

Braedon parked the truck, and Prudhoe grabbed his hand while he was removing the keys from the ignition.

"By the way, I love you...and I'm in love with you too," she said.

Braedon dropped the keys onto the floor of the truck, reached over to stroke her beautiful long hair, and then kissed her lips with deep intensity.

CHAPTER 32

Prudhoe was working hard throughout the remainder of January while her boss was trying to fill a vacancy on the floor. It meant some extra money from extended shifts and some weekend hours. Braedon was also focused on an upcoming visit to the Anchorage office by a fairly high-ranking official from Washington, DC, which was to take place in early February. Both of them were glad to get past that meeting and the hiring of an experienced nurse, who relocated from Oregon after marrying a local man. Braedon was therefore assured of being under a bit less pressure with Prudhoe's birthday coming up on February 13. He seemed determined to show her a good time and had made her promise to hold that evening free so he could take her out to celebrate in style.

By the time that Saturday had arrived, Prudhoe had splurged on a new outfit for the occasion. She had also borrowed Dika's rabbit fur coat, hat, and muff to keep warm that night. And when the time arrived for Braedon to pick her up that evening, he was almost speechless over her beauty.

"Ah, you look great. No... no, you look spectacular."

"Why thank you, Mr. Clarkson. You're not so bad yourself" Prudhoe responded with a wink. Then she puckered up her lips, colored bright red, and closed her eyes as if she was ready for a kiss, but Braedon wasn't too sure about all that.

"You okay with my messing up your lipstick?"

Prudhoe opened her eyes and said, "No, you may not mess up my lipstick. I was just testing to see if you'd really do it!"

He looked relieved as he helped her into the truck. When the passenger door was shut, she placed her muff in her lap and turned up the radio that was just teeing up Johnny Preston's "Running Bear."

"Hey, that's us. I'm little White Dove, and you're my Running Bear!" said Prudhoe.

"Well, my love for you is as big as the sky, but it's probably more like I am White Bear and you are little Running Dove," he said with a chuckle over the silly song.

Once they were on the road, Prudhoe found out they were going to a fancy hotel restaurant for her birthday dinner, then to the movies. When they arrived at the restaurant, Braedon checked their coats and seemed unable to take his eyes off Prudhoe. Perhaps it was the stunning slate-blue woven silk outfit she had chosen. The shiny material seemed to set off her dark eyes as much as it did her hourglass figure. She felt like royalty because he seated her and kept reaching for her hand across the table all evening. She didn't mind a bit; she was thoroughly enamored with her handsome date. She studied his smooth-shaven face, his thick brown hair, and his broad shoulders while he ordered dinner for the both of them.

Their time together seemed to be flying by, and before long they were nestled in their theater chairs to see the movie that was still running after many weeks in their local theater—*Ben Hur*. After seeing the film, the two agreed that it was well worth the three and a half hours in those chairs.

By eleven thirty that night, Prudhoe was getting pretty tired and was even yawning when Braedon started up the truck. Yet he insisted on staying out just a bit longer because it was a clear night, making northern lights more visible.

"Humor me, Prudy. Let's just go a few miles out of town near Eagle River Valley," pleaded Braedon.

"Oh, all right. Just not too far. Remember, we still have to drive all the way back to town, and church service will come even earlier when you're sleepy," she insisted.

The movie, the great dinner, and work-related subjects were the topics of discussion during the drive out of town. As it turned out, they didn't have to go far before seeing the dance of the aurora. Braedon pulled over to the side of the road and parked the truck. Moving a little closer to his lovely maiden, he put his arm around her. The shimmery opus swirled around like a curtain of bright colors before them.

After watching for a while in quiet awe, Braedon glanced at his watch.

"Hey, your birthday is almost over, but Valentine's Day is almost upon us. There's something I think I need to tell you right now as we hover between both of these important days. Prudy, you have been my quest ever since last summer. I found my princess alone in a very dark place and captured her upon orders of the Master of the Kingdom of Light, to whom she rightfully belonged. I think it's about time we got married so together we can face the many adventures yet to come. What do you say—will you marry me?" he asked, as he reached inside his coat pocket and pulled out a small black velvet box. As he opened it, Prudhoe found herself staring at a beautiful sapphire in gold engagement ring through watery eyes.

"Prince Braedon, I accept," whispered Prudhoe, as she reached over to kiss his waiting lips.

CHAPTER 33

Braedon stood up from his pew seat on Sunday, after the pastor asked if there were any more announcements beyond the ones he had mentioned. He then proceeded to tell everyone in the service the morning after his proposal that he and Prudhoe Bonner were to be married. It was her turn to blush when everyone clapped and the pastor congratulated the two. And after the service, Pastor Williams shook their hands and encouraged them to be married in the church. It was something that the couple had not yet discussed, but Prudhoe piped right up with a hearty "Where else?"

Braedon squeezed her hand and followed up with, "Well then, that's one decision made!"

The couple then headed out for lunch together to make some other decisions about the wedding, the most important of which was determining a date. Pulling out a small pocket calendar she'd received as a holiday gift from the hospital, Prudhoe and Braedon chose the first Saturday in summer. The weather couldn't be a consideration because it was unpredictable in Alaska after all. They also concluded that Dika would be Prudhoe's maid of honor, and Braedon's office mate Jim would be the best man. Neither one of these friends shared their faith, but the couple were determined that everyone would hear the gospel message at this wedding.

Prudhoe announced to Braedon that she'd be making her own wedding dress and asked if she could also make a vest for him to wear over a black shirt.

"Wow, no kidding? You will have time to do all that before June 25? Of course I'll wear it. After all, it's not like I own a tux or anything like that! So does this mean you want the whole affair to have an Alaskan flavor to it?"

"Yes, I guess you could say that. I'm not a fancy gal, and I want everyone to be comfortable at what will probably be a small wedding. I think our family, friends, and everyone from church should be invited. I'm guessing that means we'll spend more on feeding people than anything else," concluded Prudhoe.

"I'll bet some of the ladies at church, as well as our mothers, will want to help out with things like food and decorations," speculated Braedon.

"Oh, probably. That reminds me, I haven't called my mom to tell her yet. I spent almost an hour on the phone with Dika last night. At least now I'll have some details for her. Have you told your parents?"

"Prudy, I told them you said "yes," after preparing them for the fact that I was going to pop the question this weekend."

"You're pretty sneaky. How did they take all this?"

"They are thrilled to welcome you as a daughter. Of course, they'll drop everything to be at the wedding of their only child. Besides, I think they were beginning to worry I'd never settle down."

"Well, hadn't you ever thought about it before?" Prudhoe inquired.

"Thought about it lots of times. However, there was only one gal from high school that I ever considered marriageable material. Apparently, I was a bit slow on the uptake because by the time I figured that out, she had gotten herself engaged and then married not long after graduation. Hey, you don't need to be fishing for past loves with me. You're the only one I've ever said that to. I do love you, Prudy...now and forever."

"And I love you, Mr. Clarkson. There were plenty of times I thought I was in love before, but I really didn't know what it was. You've shown me kindness and then unconditional love...and so has God. Oh, I know you aren't God, but you surely are a man of God. I think you'll be a great guide for me in this 'land of the living,' as the Bible calls it.

"That reminds me, I have a question. As you know, I wasn't exactly an honorable gal before I repented of my ways, but do I have to keep confessing to God about that?" asked Prudhoe.

"No, that's one of the many magnificent things about God. Once our sin is confessed, he remembers it no more. We're usually the ones that keep bringing up our sins again. And another magnificent thing about him is that anyone can repent. Like I said before, the ground is level at the foot of the cross.

"Speaking of confession, here's a lie that I believed before I became a Christian—that I was the master of my life. One day it dawned on me that Jesus was the master of my destiny—or more likely, my dad informed me of that fact! I then realized that he who holds the destiny card is ultimately also the master of my life, so I might as well surrender to him. It was a tough lesson for a headstrong teen who thought he had the world by the tail."

After being dropped off that evening, Prudhoe did call her mother. Bella squealed with joy over the news. She told her daughter that she'd do all she could to help and that she really liked "her man." Dika and Patuk were also thrilled, especially when they finally got to meet Braedon by having the couple over to their place for dinner in late February. And Jim Wright seemed genuinely honored to be asked to stand with Braedon at the wedding in June.

Braedon was busy at work but also took part in the Fur Rondy sled dog race in town. He had been working with a dog team owned by the same musher who gave him Bozo. And while he didn't place, he did finish respectably, despite limited preparation time and all the distraction that was Prudhoe Bonner.

Their few months of planning and preparation took them through the thaw of spring, which all Alaskans eagerly await. The season seemed to reflect all the newness of their relationship and the anticipation of marriage. It wouldn't be long.

CHAPTER 34

Getting into her truck before heading over Dika's house after work on Friday, June 24, Prudhoe was starting to feel a bit of panic over the wedding details. She felt like she had considered everything, from picking up her mother at the airport earlier in the week to making sure that the ladies at the church had seen to every detail of the food to be served right after the wedding ceremony. However, there was one last detail she needed to put on Braedon's vest before she had Patuk deliver it to his house tonight. She would also make sure Dika had Braedon's wedding band to carry down the aisle with her the next day at eleven o'clock.

The two women were so immersed in the details that evening that Patuk finally made sandwiches for everyone at about seven o'clock because it seemed dinner had been lost in the shuffle. The excitement for tomorrow's big day was palpable. It wasn't until sometime after eight that Prudhoe got home to find her mother eating a TV dinner while watching a rerun of a *Rawhide* episode.

"Sorry to be so late, Mom. Glad you found something to eat. I would have forgotten to eat if Patuk hadn't made something for us tonight."

"I'm fine. This is actually pretty good stuff," responded Bella.

"Well, I suppose I should get to bed early tonight so I don't have bags under my eyes tomorrow," said Prudhoe.

"You're too young for that, dear, even at thirty years old. You're gonna be a beautiful Nuxalk bride tomorrow. I can hardly wait. I think marriage will suit you, Prudy."

"Well, thanks for the vote of confidence, Mother. I think marriage to a fine Christian man like Braedon is what will suit me. Now, you make yourself comfortable on that sofa bed tonight. Let me know if you need anything. I'll probably be up early with the jitters. Good night, Mom."

As Prudhoe lay in bed thinking about the wedding, seeing Braedon, and having the entire week off work for their honeymoon, she could hardly close her eyes. However, she forced herself to keep them shut and before long was fast asleep.

As predicted, Prudhoe was up around seven o'clock on her wedding day. She threw back the kitchen curtain first thing to confirm that the weatherman had predicted correctly. The sun was to be out, and the temperature would reach nearly sixty-five degrees. It was a perfect early summer day in Alaska.

Making some coffee, she tried to read the paper that landed on her front stoop, but it was hard for her to concentrate on anything this morning. After making some oatmeal for two, she dished out her portion and poured milk and some honey into the bowl. Once she had something in her stomach to stop the hunger pangs, she was off to her bedroom to inspect her wedding outfit one more time before getting into the shower. And as she exited the bathroom, she saw her mother stirring under the covers thrown onto the sofa bed.

"Good morning. I left some oatmeal in the pot for you. I thought you might want to reheat it. Coffee is on too," said Prudhoe.

With everything packed into her truck by nine thirty, Prudhoe and Bella headed down the road to the old brown church. There had been no rehearsal for this event, and as far as Prudhoe was concerned, that was the way she wanted it. It would be a short and simple ceremony that Pastor Williams would officiate. His wife would play the piano—music that Braedon selected because Prudhoe didn't feel she knew enough church music to select the right thing. In fact, this whole affair was to be casual and comfortable for all, including Bozo, who was invited to attend.

As they pulled into the dirt parking area, Prudhoe looked around to make sure they were the first ones to arrive. It appeared that the only vehicles there were that of the pastor and two friends from the hospital, who were providing the flowers as their gift to the couple. Pretty soon the ladies from the church, who would be bringing the reception food, would be arriving too.

Bella helped Prudhoe bring things into the church to a small room that was often used as the nursery during the church service. That's where Prudhoe would get ready. It was also where her suitcase was held, to be placed in Braedon's truck by the maid of honor. After the wedding, Bella would drive Prudhoe's truck back to the apartment and stay one more night. The Clarksons were staying at their son's home and would pick Bella up on Sunday to fly back to Juneau with her. Prudhoe and Braedon would leave directly for their honeymoon from the wedding reception, and Jim would take care of Bozo.

At about ten forty-five, Prudhoe was finishing up with her hair in the small room when she heard a strong knock on the door. Then she heard Braedon's voice through the door. She could feel her heart pounding faster in her chest.

"Prudy, it's me. Don't open the door; just come near to it. I'd like to say a prayer for us before the ceremony."

With her hairbrush still in hand, she moved quickly to the door. Putting her free hand on the door, she said, "I hear you."

"Father in heaven, I thank you for bringing us to this point, orchestrating everything about us along the way. Make Prudy and I into the people you want us to be for each other, and make us into the couple you want us to be for others. Make yourself at home in the center of our union. Bless us now and all the days of our lives. Amen."

Braedon heard the small "amen" coming from the other side of the door and said, "I love you, Prudy, and I can't wait to see you."

Prudhoe could hear his heavy steps departing down the small hallway toward the sanctuary. As she listened intently, she thanked God for Braedon one more time.

CHAPTER 35

The pastor's wife filled the small sanctuary with beautiful music as she played a prelude while the wedding guests found their seats. As she came to a sweet close, Pastor Williams stood front and center of the church. Braedon and his best man arose from their front row seats and stood to the left of the pastor. Both men wore black pants, shoes, and shirts with white ties. However, Braedon was sporting the soft white elk hide beaded vest that Prudhoe had made for the occasion. He stood tall with his eyes fixed on the doors of the church. The anticipation of seeing his bride was written all over his face.

By the middle of the first stanza of "Love Divine, All Loves Excelling," the doors opened, and Dika entered in her soft sky-blue dress. As Dika quickly made her way up the aisle, she placed herself at the right of the pastor.

With the doors open and the morning sun shining behind her, Prudhoe appeared from the outside steps and crossed the church threshold. Braedon stepped forward to receive his bride, and the people stood for the bride in her beautiful white elk hide beaded dress with matching soft shoes. Prudhoe wore her hair in a single loose braid down her back. Ringing her head was a crown of simple Shasta daisies laced together. In her hands, she carried a bouquet of the white daisies as well. And other than her engagement ring, the only other jewelry she wore was the copper bracelet handed down to her. The smile on her face gave away the sheer joy she felt inside. Her heart soared as she locked eyes with Braedon, who returned her smile. As she reached the front of the church, Prudhoe and Braedon locked arms and stood facing the pastor.

Williams started the service by reading a passage from Psalm 116—verses that had been chosen by the couple standing before him.

> For thou hast delivered my soul from death,
> mine eyes from tears, and my feet from falling.
> I will walk before the Lord in the land of the living.
> I believed, therefore have I spoken: I was greatly afflicted:
> I said in my haste, all men are liars.
> What shall I render unto the Lord for all his benefits toward me?
> I will take the cup of salvation, and call upon the name of the Lord.
> I will pay my vows unto the Lord now in the presence of all his people."
> From there, the pastor asked everyone to bow their heads, and he prayed:

"Lord God in heaven, hallowed is your name. We stand before you this day to witness the joining of these two children of yours together in holy matrimony. It is before you that they take these vows, and we ask that you would bless and keep them in those vows. May all who witness this sacrament praise you for their union, their steadfast love, and above all, for the picture of marriage you provide in your word. Your word is truth. Amen."

Proceeding with their vows and to the exchanging of simple gold bands, Prudhoe was on the verge of tears. She held tightly onto Braedon's big strong hand as the pastor finally uttered the words, "I now pronounce you husband and wife. You may kiss the bride."

With that, Braedon placed his arms around Prudy, and she stood on her tiptoes to receive his warm kiss. Bozo could contain himself no more and got up from his sleeping position on the floor next to Braedon's parents to join in the show of affection. With thrill and relief, the happy couple turned to exit out the door to the strains of another lovely hymn, with the tail-wagging Bozo following behind, showing off his black and white neck scarf.

Most in the little brown church stood and clapped as the couple departed into the chilly sunlight. Some threw daisies at the couple on their way out. And with just seconds alone before the stream of guests joined them in the churchyard, Prudy whispered, "I am so happy." Braedon once again took her in his arms and held her tight against his body.

The next few hours involved milling around the food tables, chatting with friends and family, and cutting the various small cakes made for them. A hand-carved canoe had been placed near the front steps of the church, where people left gifts they had brought for the newlyweds. The women placed a white shawl on Prudy so that some could pin money onto the garment as she passed by. Children played tag, and adults with cameras snapped photos of the happy couple while promising to get copies to them when they returned from the honeymoon. And as things began to wind down, Mr. and Mrs. Braedon Clarkson made their way to his truck, which now had tin cans tied to the bumper and a big Just Married sign attached above the towing hitch.

The couple waved to everyone out the back window as they drove away. Together they took great joy in seeing all the happy faces of many colors and backgrounds.

The long drive from Anchorage to Camp Denali gave Prudy and Braedon time to revel in the wedding. He told her how much he liked her dress and the vest she had made for him, praising her beadwork skills. She gushed over how handsome he looked and how meaningful the ceremony had been to her. All the while, their anticipation of finally being alone together was building.

Braedon had made arrangements for the two to spend the week in one of the small cabins at the camp at Mount McKinley National Park. The cabins were rented out by the woman who homesteaded the land years earlier. The setting was perfect, with tremendous views of the mountain and the hills filled with wildflowers at that time of the year.

After parking the truck and bringing their belongings into the small cabin, Braedon sat down on the edge of the bed and patted it as his way of inviting her to join him there. She sat down, and he grabbed her hand while looking over at her.

"Prudy, I want you to know that I've prayed for this day to arrive. I can hardly wait for us to be joined physically, but the Lord has cautioned me to continue in my patience because of the trauma you experienced last year. I suspect the first time we make love may not be easy for you, so I want you to know that I will not pressure you in any way on this matter. All I ask is that you let me know when you're ready—in your time and in your way. As with every other aspect of our marriage, we'll need to communicate our needs openly. Do you understand what I'm telling you?"

"I understand, Braedon. I appreciate your consideration, and I'll be honest... I don't know what to expect. I have had anxieties about our honeymoon, and I've prayed about them too. No matter what, just cling to this one truth—I love you and find you very attractive."

No sooner had she finished her sentence than Braedon reached over to touch her chin and tilt it toward his lips. Prudy could feel the heat within her body rising, and it wasn't long before the two were reclining on the bed. Despite inexperience, Braedon seemed to know just what to do in the moment, and Prudy allowed him to proceed. Before long, the two had had enough of their wedding clothes and began to remove them from themselves and from each other. As Braedon threw back the bedcovers to encourage her to slip inside, he sighed deeply at the sight of Prudy's naked curves. Prudy soon felt his warm strength enveloping her with his gentle but muscular embrace. Concentrating on casting out every thought except her love for Braedon, she was able to join with him in consummating their marriage before they fell asleep in each other's arms later that night.

The remainder of their honeymoon was filled with hiking, fixing meals over a campfire, praying together, resting, playing cards, and making love. Braedon even made sure that on Wednesday evening they didn't miss their Bible study by covering the same material the small group back home would be discussing. The peace and trust that they shared that week was to be a reflection of what was to come in their relationship. The two were able to spend hours together without a word spoken, while still communing with each other. Just one year later at their anniversary, Braedon presented Prudy with a poem he had written to celebrate their love. He called it "In Defense of Complacency."

> Streams of joy, confidence, honor, sympathy,
> and complacency flow freely from the union of
> two truly bonded. The last of these is not a
> disregard, but a full release and relaxation for
> the souls who know it and drink deeply thereof.
>
> Can complacency ever arrive to those who do
> not feel loved, safe, heard, or seen? Nay—it
> would never arrive for want of starting the
> journey.

EPILOGUE

Through the years, the patient and quiet love of Prudy and Braedon became a model of marriage to many—in and outside the church. In fact, just months after the Clarkson wedding, Dika and Patuk began attending the small Methodist church in Anchorage, where they eventually gave their lives to Christ. All the while, Prudy grew in her love for the scripture and eventually became a Sunday school teacher for the grade school children. Braedon often spent time counseling young men through the scriptures.

The Clarksons escaped the massive Good Friday earthquake of 1964 because Braedon had accepted a job offer in Vancouver, British Columbia. And though much of the downtown area in Anchorage was destroyed, there were very few deaths. Dika and Patuk suffered major damage to their place, but they lived to tell of it, as well as the process of urban renewal that came later. The little brown church where the Clarksons married survived too, though much of the structure required reinforcement.

In his new position with Chuck West's touring company, Braedon was able to share his love and knowledge of Alaska with the patrons. He thoroughly enjoyed working for Westours, the first to operate cruise ships in Alaskan waters since the old steamship days. He later became a manager when the company became Cruise West. That change eventually took the family to Seattle, Washington where they remained.

Prudy stayed with her nursing career even after their first child was born in 1962 by working part-time. Their second son came along not long after they moved to Canada in 1964. And finally a baby girl arrived in 1967, born at Swedish Hospital in Seattle where Prudy worked weekend shifts.

Since the couple had taken Prudy's mother with them in all their moves, Bella was very helpful and involved in the care of the children as they grew. In fact, she gave up drinking altogether as she poured herself into her grandchildren. And it was with great joy that the Clarksons welcomed Bella into the family of God when she gave her life to the Lord Jesus prior to her passing in 1975.

Prudy returned to full-time nursing in the early 1980s as one by one the children began to go off to college. As a lifelong learner, she had maintained her skills and even went on in formal education at the University of Washington. Her nursing degree enabled her to move into the nurse management ranks, leading to her becoming the director of nursing services at a public district hospital in her area. Many young nurses were mentored and taught by their black- and silver-haired leader, who carried herself erect and exhibited great wisdom. Her successful career drew to a close in 1995 when she was diagnosed with an aggressive form of breast cancer that ultimately took her life later that year. Braedon held her hand in her last hours as his beloved Prudy assured him that she no longer feared death as she did before she knew Jesus.

A widower at age sixty-eight, Braedon chose to retire from his executive management role at the Holland America Line, which had earlier bought out Cruise West. He never remarried because of his eternal love for Prudy. With another decade to enjoy his hobbies of fishing and hunting—as well as his six grandchildren—Bracdon passed away in his sleep in 2005 at the age of seventy-eight.

No greater love.

ALSO FROM RAYANNE SINCLAIR

When Anne Ledwell graduates from Penn State University in 1977, her parents gift her a trip to the British Isles. She's looking forward to a break from her frustrating job search, but the last thing she expects is to fall into the arms of a handsome Scottish balladeer.

In 1980, Katerina Steiner goes to Europe to reconnect with her only living relatives. After a brief romantic encounter with an intriguing fellow tourist in Paris, Katerina returns home to find her former beau is hoping to recapture her attention. How will she choose?

In 1960, Page Holden leaves her small-town life behind to pursue her dream of becoming a concert pianist. Enter into her journey – because love has a melody of its own.

Available for Kindle and in print wherever books are sold.

Visit Rayanne online at http://rayannesinclair.com/

CPSIA information can be obtained at www.ICGtesting.com
Printed in the USA
BVOW02s1734170216

437031BV00001B/44/P

9 780989 750264